ABOUT THIS BOOK

He looks at me like he wants to own me. I'm not one to be owned. He's not one to be denied.

I never understood the draw of the biker scene. In fact, knowing what I did, I hated it. But Pops swore if anyone could keep me protected, it was the Swords of the Infernal Night in New Orleans. A band of supernatural criminals who think women are possessions, if you ask me. And they haven't kept us safe. Pops is dead, but his murderers are after me, all because my inner kelpie became the first in generations to grow a horn. My name is Reyna Moreno, and yep, I'm a damn unicorn. Which makes me more valuable than the Hope Diamond.

To keep me protected, my brother hauls me off to some gods-forsaken town in Colorado where another SIN chapter "takes us in." Takes me prisoner is more like it. It wouldn't be so bad if my sexy-as-hell warden wasn't such an ass. And wasn't only a biker, but one of the MC's leaders.

He looks at me like he wants to own me. I'm not one to be owned. He's not one to be denied.

They call him Savage for a reason. He's a hellhound and a savage beast. And he would be my undoing . . . but maybe I could be his salvation.

HAVENWOOD FALLS SIN & SILK BOOKS

Taming the Beast by Nadirah Foxx

Plans Laid Bare by JD Nelson

Shift of Fate by Victoria Escobar

Stolen Wishes by Victoria Flynn

Damned Allure by Justine Winter

Savage Salvation by Kristie Cook

Dark Seduction by Michele G. Miller & R.K. Ryals

Soul Laid Bare by JD Nelson

Stray With Me by E.J. Fechenda

Chase the Flames by Desiree Lafawn

Flirting With Death by Nadirah Foxx

Also try the signature line, Havenwood Falls, the historical paranormal line, Legends of Havenwood Falls, and stories from the local supernatural college in Sun & Moon Academy.

Stay up to date at www.HavenwoodFalls.com

ALSO BY KRISTIE COOK

SOUL SAVERS

Recommended Reading Order:

A Demon's Promise

An Angel's Purpose

Genesis: A Soul Savers Novella

Dangerous Devotion

Dark Power

Sacred Wrath

Unholy Torment

Fractured Faith

Age of Angels Part I: Awakened

Age of Angels Part II: Lost

Age of Angels Part III: Marked

Prophecy of the Wolves: (A Soul Savers Tie-In Novella)

Wonder: A Soul Savers Collection of Holiday Short Stories & Recipes

KNIGHTS OF SOULS AND SHADOWS

Knights of Souls and Shadows, Book 1

HAVENWOOD FALLS

Recommended Reading Order:

Forget You Not

Lose You Not

Break Me Not

The Collector: Awakening

Savage Salvation (Sin & Silk)

Sun & Moon Academy Book One: Fall Semester

Sun & Moon Academy Book Two: Fall Semester

The Winged & the Wicked (with T.V. Hahn)

Havenwood Falls Short Story Anthology 2018

Havenwood Falls Short Story Anthology 2019

Havenwood Falls Short Story Anthology 2020

Havenwood Falls Short Story Anthology 2021

Havenwood Falls Spring Anthology 2022

Havenwood Falls Sunset Anthology 2022

BOOK OF PHOENIX

The Space Between

The Space Beyond

The Space Within

SAVAGE SALVATION

A HAVENWOOD FALLS SIN & SILK NOVELLA

KRISTIE COOK

To the one who inspired Savage
First you made me see stars at the Stargate, next we rode hard across the
Dothraki Sea, and then you took me to deep, dark, and very wet places . . .
all the way to Atlantis . . .
Because you make a lady think all the naughty things, this book is
dedicated to you, my fictional husband, Jason Momoa

SWORDS OF THE INFERNAL NIGHT

SIN   MC

COLORADO

CHAPTER 1

*T*he service came to a close, and everyone stood, the metal chairs creaking almost as loudly as all the leather in the room. I stared at the focal point of the space—the gleaming wooden box dressed in flowers flowing over its edges—as several pairs of heavy boots thudded toward it. At the direction of some guy I'd spoken with only briefly, the six men gathered around the box and lifted.

I stood, turned, and hurried down the aisle, out the other way, my heels clicking in loud echoes on the tile floor as I crossed the lobby. The door nearly knocked over a group of girls when I threw it open, and they yelped as they jumped out of the way. They bitched and moaned, straightening their skin-tight dresses that barely covered the goods. The skanks had no respect. This was a funeral, for mother's sake, and they were dressed like they were auditioning for their next role in a porn.

"Rey." The deep, familiar voice called after me, but I ignored him, heading for my car. I slid into the two-seater Benz, but didn't quite get the door closed before Niall grabbed it. "Reyna. Don' be like this." His Scottish accent came thickly when he was mad.

"Go to hell."

"C'mon, sis."

My jaw clenched. "Don't call me that. You're not my brother."

1

"For all intents and purposes—"

"What do you want?" I pressed the Start button, and the engine purred to life.

"You're coming to the cemetery, right?"

"Of course I am," I muttered.

My gaze stayed forward, but in my periphery, I saw his thick beard bob as he nodded, then he closed the door. I inhaled deeply and blew the air out slowly, refusing to shed a tear. Unable to, if I was honest. I hadn't yet been able to cry for the man who'd been like an uncle to me, who'd taken a sort of fatherly role when my own had passed. After another deep breath, I followed the procession to the cemetery, also known as the city of the dead. The above-ground tombs and mausoleums lined the pathways like buildings lined the city streets.

Pops didn't get a traditional New Orleans funeral. No jazz music and parading through the streets. Besides all the other reasons, the club wouldn't allow it. Like they should have any say. The New Orleans chapter of the Swords of the Infernal Night motorcycle club, SIN or SIN-NO for short, shouldn't have a say at all in our lives, as far as I was concerned. In fact, if it were up to me, this would be the last time I'd see any of them. Pops trusted them all with our lives, and he lost his for it. I would never trust any of them again.

Not that I ever did in the first place.

I liked to think Niall, who had been like a brother to me, looked out for us, but the rest of them? To hell with them all. They didn't do their job.

I went for a drive once I made sure Pops was in his final resting place, two Harleys rumbling loudly behind me the whole time. Supposedly the two members of SIN were there to guard me, but I couldn't fathom what they thought they could do from back there if I were attacked. It wasn't like the people after me could be taken down with a bullet. If that were the case, Pops would still be alive.

My phone rang, and I ignored it. It persisted until I finally hit the answer button on the steering wheel.

"Reyna," Niall's Scottish lilt came over the car speakers. "Come on home, lass."

"That's not my home." I hadn't been to my home in months.

"Well then, come to *my* home."

"Why? So you can make me a prisoner?"

"We need to talk. Plans have been made."

"Screw you and your plans, Niall. Look where it got us. Pops is—" I hiccupped before continuing— "dead, and I—"

"You're goin' to be okay. It's been arranged. Just come to the club house. You know I hate talking on these things. Especially about this."

He had a point there. We were practically screaming "here I am" at all those who wanted to find me.

"Don't make us force you," he added.

I blew out a sigh. "Fine. I'm on my way. But one thing, Niall."

"What?"

"I'm nobody's bitch. Not yours. Not anyone's. And I'm certainly not an old lady or anybody's property. So stop treating me like I am."

"I'm not. I'm treating you with concern for your safety, which is my job, my qu—"

"Don't you fucking say it." I disconnected the call before he said the word that made me want to hurl every time I heard it. Gah! A shudder ran through me. I'd rather he call me sis or anything else than the word he'd been about to say.

The two bikers followed me like puppy dogs through the streets into an industrial area a few blocks from the French Quarter. As soon as I turned in to the driveway, the gate across it started rolling to the side, and I pulled in. The compound was lit up in more ways than one. The club was obviously having some kind of celebration of life ceremony—just another excuse for everyone to drink until they passed out. I knew this was supposed to be a big honor, since Pops had been a friend of the club but never an actual member, but it felt like salt followed by tequila in my wounds. And not in the good way. Drunk members, friends of the club, hangers-on, and groupies whooped and hollered from inside the brightly lit main building, and the moans and grunts of people fornicating were scattered across the grounds outside. It had only just grown dark. It was going to be a long night.

Niall opened my door for me before I even cut the engine. He stood there in loose jeans, motorcycle boots, a black T-shirt, and his leather vest, called a cut in MC terms, covered in patches. One of them said "Torq," his road name—what everyone here called him. He angled his dark head toward a smaller building to the right of the main one before turning, the large patch of a skull with its head impaled by a rose-wrapped sword staring back at me.

I followed silently, surprised to be heading toward the small structure. The big house was where some of the members lived and where Pops and I had been staying the last several months. It also housed the party area, with a long bar, a couple of pool tables, and a few threadbare couches stained with substances I didn't want to think too hard about or I'd need to bleach my brain. It stunk, pun intended, having supernatural senses when you lived where there was practically an orgy every other night. This small building, though, served as the club's church—where they held their meetings and did their business.

I didn't like the idea of being a piece of their business, but at least they had the decency to invite me in on the subject this time around. Well, not really invite. It'd still been more like an order, even if it had been delivered by my so-called brother. And I was only assuming that was what was going on—that this was about me. Pops may have been a friend of the club, but I'd never been all that friendly with them. In fact, I'd always made my disdain quite clear. And now Pops was dead, and they needed to figure out what to do with me. Throwing me out would be disrespectful to Pops's memory. And while I thought of them as no more than criminal scum, I couldn't deny that the club did have a code, and respect was important to them.

And it wasn't just about Pops.

They'd have to deal with kelpies worldwide—some of whom were already in town for the funeral—if the club tried anything stupid with me. Considering the number of kelpies in the various chapters of the club, that'd create a lot of extra tension for the SIN president to deal with. Of course, he was known for doing such things when he was bored, and I was pretty sure he'd grown bored of me a long time ago when I refused to screw him.

"Reyna, come in and have a seat," Prez said when Niall and I

4

entered the building. I paid him little notice, but I could feel his gaze undressing me as he motioned toward a room with a large conference table surrounded by a dozen or more chairs. The dim lighting from a table lamp in the corner created shadows, the far end of the room doused in obsidian darkness—but I could sense the people there. Or beings, anyway. As I entered, a hint of sulfur burned my nose, but then it was followed by a scent that was musky, warm, and mouth-watering, making my belly tighten and my thighs squeeze together. *What the hell?* Whoever was back there, they definitely weren't human and not kelpie, either—not my kind here to protect me.

Not that my people were a huge threat to most of the SIN members in any chapter, including those here. They were all supernaturals, many of whom were a lot more badass than people who shifted into horses. Unless there was a body of water around and the other supe couldn't swim, kelpies were mostly dangerous only to humans.

Except me.

I was the first in many generations of our kind to grow a horn. One single horn, right out of the top of my forehead. Yep, I was a damn unicorn. The silver horn had first broken through when I was twelve, only a few months after my first shift. It'd hurt like a bitch, and even in my human form, I still had a scar at my hairline, barely visible under all my curls. I'd only been able to shift a few times in the thirteen years since then, because as soon as word got out, my life was endangered. From my horn to my tears to the hairs in my mane and tail, I had way too many valuable parts. Parts that some would love to harvest.

Hunters came for me almost right away, in my home country of Brazil, and killed my parents. Pops, who wasn't really related but had been like an uncle to me, escaped with Niall and me, whisking us off to America. Niall had always been like an adopted brother, coming to us as an orphan when I was nine and he was supposedly fifteen. I didn't learn until we were found again a year ago that he was much, much older—kelpies, like all fae, lived very long lives while retaining youthful appearances, especially when we used glamour—and that he'd been groomed all his life to be a warrior to protect the future queen. He'd been sent to Brazil when a fae Seer prophesized that the next kelpie queen would come from our small South American town. We hadn't known then, before I'd ever even shifted, that this queen was me. Because for some reason in kelpie law, the one with the horn ruled.

I really did not want to rule.

At least, I didn't want to rule a smattering of supernaturals that hadn't been a true herd in generations. The kelpies had escaped to the earthly realm during a devastating war in our Faerie homeland many centuries ago. They stayed together in Scotland for a while, but rifts over time sent more and more away, and after the last unicorn queen died, what remained of the herd scattered. If the need arose, they'd be compelled to come together once again for me, but could they ever be a herd again? Especially since so many had joined a different kind of herd—the SIN MC? Whom would they truly be loyal to if it came down to it? Me and each other or their patch?

Hopefully, the need would never arise.

As I walked farther into the room as though drawn to the far end by that delicious smell, annoyance doused the desire when I noticed my designer luggage piled by the doorway. I turned on Niall, Prez, and Chintz, the VP, while trying to tamper my anger—not because they were kicking me out, but because they'd dared to touch my personal property.

"Not wasting any time, I see." I gave them a saccharine smile. "No worries, though. I wasn't planning on staying anyway."

Niall reached out, cupping my elbow and leading me toward a chair. "Sit, Rey."

"I'm not a dog." My patience was waning. Someone at the far end of the room snickered.

Niall sighed. "Sit down and listen. Like I said, we have a plan. It's all taken care of."

None of the bikers sat, so neither did I. "I don't need your plan."

"Ya do," Niall insisted.

"He's right," Prez said, his voice deep and full of promise of dark, ugly things. His beady eyes were barely visible behind all his dark facial hair, but I felt them on me, the sensation like cold slime. He crossed his log-thick arms over his barrel chest. "The hunters know you're here this very second. Our guys followed two of them who were following you."

"They're dead," Chintz said flatly. He leaned his thin yet sinewy arms on the back of one of the chairs, also appraising me as I let that sink in. My insides felt sick, but I refused to squirm in their presence.

"You're willing to go to war over me, yet you're kicking me out?" I asked.

Chintz shrugged. "We've gone to war for lesser reasons."

"We swore an oath to Pops," Prez said as a better explanation. "We don't go back on our word."

"Yet you're kicking me out," I repeated, my hand gesturing toward my suitcases.

"We're sendin' you to a safe place," Niall said.

Every muscle in my body tensed up. "You're *sending* me to a safe place? What does that mean? You're not sending me anywhere! Who do you think you are?"

"Reyna!" Niall barked, and I'd never heard him say my name so sharply. "You need to listen. It's for your own god damn safety."

My ample chest heaved as I tried to regain control of my anger. My inner beast had awakened. I'd learned long ago how to contain her, but she always showed interest when my emotions rose, hoping I'd finally let her break free. This would be the absolute worst time to indulge her, especially with strangers in the room, so I forced her to settle down and go back to sleep. Crossing my arms over my breasts, I cocked my head, my only indication that I was listening.

"A SIN chapter in Colorado has agreed to provide you protection," Prez said.

My jaw dropped. "*Colorado?* No way in hell!"

"They'll take you in, under the wards of their town," Prez continued gruffly, ignoring my outburst.

"It's a small town in the mountains," Niall added. "I bet you'll love it."

I'll bet I won't.

Someone on the far end emerged from the darkness—over six feet tall, sandy brown hair, wearing sunglasses—at night, inside, in the dark—and a leather cut with a small patch that said Pirate and another under it that said President. That vague hint of sulfur wafted to my nose. Demon, perhaps?

"Our town isn't like anyplace else," he said, his voice deep and raspy. "There's no safer place."

"No offense, Mr. . . ."

"Pirate," he said.

"Mr. Pirate."

"Just. *Pirate*," the stranger growled.

I blinked, suppressing the urge to roll my eyes. "Okay, no offense, *Pirate*, but these assholes here couldn't protect us, so what makes you think you can?"

That snicker sounded again from the dark end of the room.

"And I can't go all the way to Colorado," I hurried on, because my question had been rhetorical and I didn't want them thinking they needed to answer it. "I have a business to run, which these dumb shits seem to have forgotten."

I turned back to Niall and Prez with a raised brow.

No, I didn't want to rule a kingdom. But I did want to rule an empire.

And I'd already been on my way to building it with my plus-size fashion and lifestyle blog and specialty lingerie designs when the hunters discovered our location and we had to go into hiding a year ago. That made running a business a little difficult, and I knew my clients were almost out of patience. Good thing for me that they loved my designs too much to completely give up on me.

But disappearing to a small mountain town in Colorado where they probably didn't even have indoor plumbing, let alone internet service? That would be a career killer.

"Your laptop's packed," Niall said. "All your business stuff is. You've already been running it remotely for a year. You haven't lost any business yet, have you?"

"I haven't gained any, either," I sniped back. My brain knew it wasn't Niall's or anyone else's fault that the hunters were after me. Somewhere deep down I also knew it wasn't his or the MC's fault that I'd been found. But damn it, it was their fault that Pops was dead and we were even having this discussion.

All I wanted was to be in my own bed in my own home, preparing for tomorrow's work day like any normal person. Just like I had been before the hunters had discovered my general location, and now they'd come way too close. If Niall and the MC had done their jobs properly, I could have at least had some semblance of my old life. We definitely wouldn't be discussing some trip to Colorado or the future of my business that wasn't looking so promising anymore. So repressing my anger wasn't easy.

Besides, if I didn't stay angry, the grief would kick in.

"Don' be difficult, Rey," Niall practically begged, his accent thicker than usual. He knew I had a soft spot for it. "Yeh know yeh can't stay here, love. Yeh can't leave this compound and expect to live. And how many people here are you goin' to let die for yeh?"

I scowled. He knew exactly what buttons to push.

"Yer life, yer people's lives, these people's lives—no matter how much yeh don't like 'em—they're more importan' than anythin', aren't they?" he continued, tilting his head as he stared me down with piercing sapphire eyes, challenging me to argue further.

I opened my mouth to do just that, because I was stubborn like that. There had to be another way. No, I wouldn't let anyone here die while protecting me. Niall was the only one who had any kind of place in my heart, but just because I didn't like the MC and their crowd didn't mean I wanted them dead. Especially not for me.

But Colorado couldn't possibly be our only choice.

Those words were on the tip of my tongue when the other figure stepped out of the shadows at the far end of the room, that delicious scent wafting toward me again.

And if my body's reaction meant anything, any other options had just been wiped off the table.

CHAPTER 2

"*P*rez, time's about up." His voice was deep, gravelly, rough —the sound guttural, feral, like an orgasmic groan that made my belly drop and flip.

He spoke to Pirate, stepping up next to the other chapter's president, but I somehow knew that behind the mirrored sunglasses, his focus was completely on me. And I felt it in every cell of my body that lit up like a flipping Christmas tree.

He was possibly the tallest, broadest man I'd ever seen. I'd been around supernaturals all my life. An outlaw one-percenter club full of them for half my life. I was used to extra-large males, but this one made everyone else in the room look average. Made me feel small. He stood nearly a foot taller than me, and I was five foot ten. His shoulders and arms were perfectly proportional to his height—in other words, massive. Muscular. But not competitive bodybuilder type. More like bodyguard type. Much more intimidating than a gym rat.

His hair hung loosely, waving down past his shoulders, dark on top and growing lighter toward the ends. Dark brows arched sharply upward at the outsides, giving him a naturally mean look. He wore a closely cropped beard, yet his full lips were still quite noticeable. At least, I was noticing them and thinking way too much about what they might taste like . . . feel like.

I forced my gaze downward, trying to break contact, but then I wondered just how close to perfect his chest and abs were . . . and if his dick was like the rest of him—big and full of promised poundings. *Reyna!* Even as I mentally scolded myself for such uncharacteristic, wayward thoughts, my thighs clenched and my panties dampened.

His nostrils flared. He growled quietly.

"Let's get the package and go," he snarled at Pirate.

And then he had to open that perfect mouth and remind me what he was.

The focus of my gaze widened outward, taking in the black T-shirt and leather cut. A damn biker. To him and everyone else here, I was nothing more than property and a job—not a woman or sentient being with a brain and heart and soul, but a thing to possess and control. How could I have forgotten? I'd nearly been willing to do anything and go anywhere with this beautiful lowlife before me. Pheromones. It had to be the pheromones clouding my judgment. I'd do well to never forget again exactly what he was.

His name patch said Savage and his title was VP.

Savage.

I bet he's a savage in bed.

My mind drifted again to more naughty thoughts. My panties were no longer damp. They were soaked.

Damn it. Stop it, Rey!

Disgust filled me—disgust with myself. I'd never had thoughts like this for anyone, especially not a biker. My fantasies centered on boardroom executives dressed in suits, whisking me off on private jets to Milan for dinner and London for a show. And my reality—well, we'll just say it lacked any of the above. There was little reality in that area of my life, a couple of boyfriends here and there, each quickly scared away by Niall, if not my body type.

"If we're doing this, we gotta do it now, Torq," Pirate said.

"We're definitely doing this," Niall replied.

"The hell we are," I said, although I could hear the conviction in my voice wasn't as strong as it had been two minutes ago. Savage had awoken my inner beast in a way she'd never been woken before. Curiosity aroused us—in more ways than one.

Biker, Rey. You. Don't. Do. Bikers. Another voice, this one dripping with sarcasm, piped up, *You don't do anyone.*

"Brothers, we need the room for a minute," Niall said as he glared at me.

The bikers shuffled out of the door with a gruff "hurry up" growled by one of them.

Niall stepped in front of me, lifting my chin with his finger as he angled his head to look me in the eye with his blue ones, extra bright among all the dark hair on his head and face. "The club went out of their way for us, Rey. These guys from Colorado don't have to do shite for you or me. They owe us nothin'. But when there are supernatural beings to hide and protect, they're the ones who can do it like no one else."

"Then why didn't Pops go to them?" I asked, one side of my mouth curling back with skepticism.

"Because he didn't know them, and he did know this chapter. We've known SIN-NO as long as we've been in the States, Rey. You know that. The Colorado chapter is different, though. Nobody knows why. But when you're in trouble and they offer to take you in, that's something you don't turn your nose up at. Not even you, lass. You can't afford to. Our people need you to remain alive and well. And you can't build your empire if you're dead."

I turned my head, just enough to free myself from his grip. "Maybe I just need to sneak off by myself and find a way to lay low. The hunters won't expect me to be on my own. They'll be looking for an entourage."

"First of all, over my dead fookin' body. You daft? Second, there won't be an entourage out of here. Third, if the guys couldn't protect Pops, what makes you think you can protect your own arse? And last but not least, if something happened to you, Pops woulda died in vain. Your parents, too. Is that what you want, lass?" He lifted a single eyebrow.

I scowled in return. "Of course not."

"Then let's go skiing, love," he said with a half-smile, before signaling for the others.

They filed in, their boots scuffing heavily along the floor.

"Are we doing this?" Pirate asked, and Niall nodded. He looked over at Savage. "Let 'em know."

The big guy's big fingers tapped on a phone that looked like a toy in his oversized hand. For the next several minutes, it became quickly obvious that they'd carefully crafted some complicated strategy to extricate me from the MC's compound without being seen. While they put it in action, I changed out of my funeral clothes, into black jeans and a black hoodie that Niall handed me. Lovely. Then they took my phone with the promise to get me a burner down the road and said my computer and tablet had already been scanned and double-checked for bugs and tracking devices.

"We're not fookin' around this time," Niall said when I balked at handing my phone over. "We messed up once and look what hap'n."

The hunters had first discovered us because someone had sensed me at an industry show, and a photographer for a fashion magazine had caught my face on camera just right, able to confirm what they sensed. After that, it was just a matter of following the paper trail—well, electronic trail, consisting of my blog, business contacts, and eventually my ISP and phone. I hadn't been to a show since, which wasn't helping my career at all.

I reluctantly fished my phone out of my purse, glad that everything I needed on it was safely stored in the cloud. Prez took it and pocketed it.

"Let's ride," Pirate said, once they ensured everything was in place.

"I'm going with Prez and Chintz on a decoy run," Niall explained to me, and when I opened my mouth to argue, he added, "But I'll catch up. I'm not sending you out there alone. You can't get rid of my arse that easily."

I'd never felt like a piece of property more than when I was hidden in the back of a cargo truck with a bunch of boxes, and I swore when this was over, I'd never have anything to do with these assholes again. As I crouched in the dark corner of the metal box, I lumped Niall in as one of those assholes. What the hell had he been thinking?

We drove for what felt like hours, but I couldn't be sure from my corner of the truck. My butt was numb, and I had to pee, so it'd been a while. Finally, the truck stopped, and the back door rolled up. Pirate climbed in and picked his way back to me, holding out a coat, a hat, and sunglasses.

"Right over here," he said once I was disguised, leading me out of the U-Haul truck and to an older RV.

We were behind a row of semis in the dark corner of a truck stop. I hesitated at the step leading to the door of the RV. I didn't know this guy from anyone. How did I know he wasn't one of the hunters or about to turn me in to them?

"We gotta ride," Pirate said, urging me upward.

While he was a biker—president of his club, no less—there was something calming about him. Authoritative, rough, and pushy, but I sensed something else that made me think he might have been a father. For some reason, believing that brought a bit of ease, but I still remained apprehensive, my foot on the step and my hand reaching for the door handle, but unable to move. Pirate sighed behind me, then held a phone up to my ear.

"It's okay." Niall's voice came through the earpiece. "I can see you on the step—I'm that close. We thought you'd be more comfortable in the rig."

Swallowing the small lump in my throat, I went up and inside, relieved to find a working toilet.

As I came out of the bathroom, that mouthwatering scent hit my nose. Savage had just come in, his large body filling the space at the front of the RV.

"I'm driving," he growled, grabbing the kid in the driver's seat by the collar and yanking him out.

"You?" the kid said with a laugh, grabbing his cut from the passenger seat and slipping it on. His patch read *Prospect*. "You're gonna drive and not ride?"

Savage only grunted as he draped his cut over the seat back before sliding in behind the wheel.

"What about your bike?" the kid asked.

"You ride it."

The kid's jaw dropped. Mine nearly did, too. For a biker, that was like saying, "Here, have a go with my old lady."

"Don't make me regret it," Savage snarled.

"But . . . I was supposed to drive her." He jerked his head toward me.

"No. Fucking. Way."

The kid paused for another moment, then hurried out the door. I remained frozen for at least a minute, then figured I'd better sit down. I'd just started to move when Pirate came stomping up the steps and through the door.

"This wasn't the plan," he barked at Savage.

"It is now." He didn't even look up at his president.

Pirate glanced at me, then turned back to Savage. "You can protect her out there just as well. Probably better."

"Nope."

A silent beat passed and then another before Pirate sighed loudly. "What the fuck ever." He jogged down the steps and banged on the side of the rig. "Let's ride."

The door closed at the same time the engine turned over.

"Sit down and buckle up," Savage said, the sound low and rumbly. The man had permanent bedroom voice. Unfortunately, his tone seemed to be permanent asshole tone.

I hurried into the passenger seat and pulled on my seat belt. He seemed to be staring straight forward, but I was sure behind those sunglasses—yeah, he still wore them, even at night and inside the rig —he was peering over at me. I could *feel* it. The sensation dissipated when we began rolling forward, toward the truck stop's exit. Motorcycles rumbled in the distance. I watched as four turned onto the main road a hundred yards ahead of us, but there were more, somewhere behind us.

"You gave up your bike," I said, the curiosity killing me. Savage replied with some kind of confirming noise. "Why?"

"Doin' my job."

I turned in my seat to look at him. "Being my chauffeur is your job? Wasn't that the other guy's job?"

"I don't trust him to do it right."

"You don't trust him to drive this grandpa-mobile, but you trust him with your *bike*?"

He turned to look at me—I knew for sure he was now—and it was more than a stolen glance. He was staring at me, as though appraising me. The weight of his gaze was warm . . . and tingly. His nostrils flared before he turned back toward the road, shifting in his seat.

"I don't trust him to protect you. Not like I can." The way he said those last four words made me feel like protecting me was somehow more than a job for him. I sensed ownership in his voice, but not in a me-biker-you-old-lady-grunt-grunt Neanderthal kind of way. More like in a you're-important-to-me-and-I-will-die-for-you kind of way. Which was absolutely ridiculous. I nearly snorted at myself for even having the thought.

Even if he didn't feel that, I could tell he felt something. This sexual tension in the air couldn't have been completely one-sided. Could it?

"I still don't get it," I pressed, trying to feel him out. When he didn't encourage me to continue, I did anyway. "Your president said this wasn't the plan. That you could protect me better out there. Yet you changed the plan." I paused, but he still didn't say anything. "And gave up your bike." I waited again. "For me."

He blew out a harsh breath. "She's not my bike," he snapped.

"Oh." That was unexpected.

"I just bought her on the way to get you. *My* bike's at home."

"So this is a backup?"

"A new project. And you—" He looked over at me again and slid his sunglasses down his nose. I couldn't tell the color of his eyes in the glow of the dash lights, but I could see a very prominent reddish-orange glow before he quickly pushed the glasses back up. And suddenly so much made sense.

"You're a hellhound," I said with understanding. The sunglasses were a protective measure—if a human and even some supes looked into his eyes three times, they could die. Sooner, if he wanted. I'd just been given time number one.

"And you're my charge."

Hellhounds were extremely protective of those put in their care. That must have been what I'd sensed from him, and nothing else. The sexual tension really was one-sided.

I turned to stare out the side window, into the inky night.

"There's a bed in back," Savage growled after a while. "Go sleep."

Don't tell me what to do. Instinct made me want to argue, but the more I thought about it, the more a bed sounded nice. After another hour or so of riding in silence, I made my way to the back, where I could breathe more normally without his scent invading my senses. The tightness between my legs loosened, and it didn't take long for the motion of the RV and the sound of the road to lull me to sleep.

I awoke to the sound of a quiet song and rolled over, getting my bearings. Savage still drove, though the sky had lightened quite a bit outside. It was his voice singing, and it was mesmerizing.

After stopping to pee in the tiny bathroom, I stumbled up to the front seat. Desert spread out before us.

"Where are we?" I asked as I glanced at my watch. 6:30 a.m. We'd been driving for nearly twelve hours.

"Texas panhandle." Savage glanced over at me. "What the fuck is that?" I looked around, my eyes still bleary and not seeing what he was. "On your wrist."

I held it up, confused. "My FitBit."

"God damn it," he growled, and somehow, in one quick motion, he managed to jerk it off my wrist, roll down the window, and throw it out in the road.

"Hey, asshole! What the hell did you do that for?" I yelled.

"Tracking—" He never finished his statement.

Something slammed into the side of the RV, and we went rolling.

17

CHAPTER 3

*T*he vehicle rolled twice before coming to rest on its side—on my side. I landed smooshed up against the window, something extremely heavy weighing me down. I wiggled just enough to see what I was dealing with, perhaps a seat and hopefully not the engine.

Nope.

A hard-lined, rugged, sexy as hell face hovered only inches from mine, his hair curtaining the space between us. We stared at each other for a long moment, both of our chests heaving against the other. The weight of his body on mine suddenly felt completely different, and my own began to respond. Swallowing, I forced myself to break the hold, cutting my eyes to the side to see the cracked windshield.

"You hurt?" Savage asked, his breath warm and smoky on my face, but his tone harsh as usual.

I took a quick mental inventory of all my parts. I had no sharp pains anywhere, and anything less, such as bruising, I didn't think I'd notice at the moment. My body was too busy feeling other things. Stupid body.

"I'm fine. You?"

I swore the corner of his lip began to curl the slightest bit before he went stoic again. "Fine."

He maneuvered his way off of me, and my body immediately missed his. *Stop it, Rey! More important things to worry about.*

With one thrust of both feet, Savage shoved the windshield out. He climbed outside, then turned back toward me. "Glamour yourself."

I blinked. "What?"

"You're fae. Do I need to spell it out?"

"I . . . uh . . ." I stammered. Kelpie were from Faerie, which technically made us a type of fae, but we weren't like faeries or elves. Did he not know what I was or just not know the difference? I had some glamouring abilities, but nothing like theirs. I did the best I could, lightening my tan skin and dark hair, straightening the kinks into waves.

"You can't do better than that?" he grumbled, and I shook my head as he reached his hand in and grabbed my wrist, pulling me out of the wreckage.

I jumped down from the prone RV onto the asphalt of a barren stretch of highway in the middle of the desert. There wasn't much there to hide behind besides cacti and some low brush, but I could smell the attackers—dark fae. Possibly Unseelie, but I couldn't be sure. Faerie was home to many dark kinds. Were these the same hunters who had killed Pops? Nobody had said anything about dark fae before. If they weren't the same, then the word of my whereabouts had spread. I was in more danger than I realized.

A figure streaked from the shoulder toward us. Savage jumped in its way, tackling it to the ground. They rolled around the road, all snarls and growls, snapping teeth and fists on flesh. They quickly came to a stop, Savage jumping to his feet and bringing the attacker with him. His large hands, now clawed, were gripped around the fae's head, squeezing it like a melon, the man's eyes bulging from their sockets. Savage's shades had come off in the tussle, and he stared directly in the fae's face, dark gray smoke swirling into the air from his skin. Savage's growl turned into a howl. My head felt like it was about to explode from the deadly sound that could only come from Hell, and I clamped my hands over my ears. The fae had no way to defend himself, and he crumpled, held up only by the hellhound's partially shifted hands.

19

"Savage!" I screamed, my heart pounding from the scene unfolding before me.

His howl fell silent.

"We could use him," another voice rumbled, and Savage let the fae drop to the ground, his chest barely moving with shallow breaths.

In all the commotion, I hadn't noticed the others' arrival. Several motorcycles circled us, their riders already standing in defensive positions, guns out.

"Get her out of here, Savage," Pirate growled. He'd been the one to stop his VP from killing the fae. Smoke rose from his skin, too, smelling of brimstone. Pirate was also a hellhound.

Savage stomped toward me and, taking my wrist again, tugged me toward the kid from the RV and the massive bike next to him.

"No bitch seat," the kid pointed out.

Savage growled, while I suppressed my own. Why did they have to call the back seat that?

"Take mine," Niall called from the other side of the circle as a jolt of energy slammed into the RV, missing me by less than a yard.

Guns started firing into the desert, as if they could hurt the fae. Although, if they used iron bullets, maybe they could at least slow the hunters down. We ran for Niall and his bike. Savage swung his leg over the motorcycle.

"If anything happens to her—" Niall began.

"I got her," Savage barked.

"Niall?" I turned toward him. As mad as I'd been, I couldn't bear for anything to happen to him. "What about you?"

"We'll be right behind you, lass. Now go!" He practically shoved me onto the bike, which was already rumbling under Savage.

I hesitated, unsure of the mental stability of the man whose hands I was about to put my life in. He'd just nearly killed a man! Not even a man—a fae. They weren't exactly easy to kill. When another blast of fae magic soared right by us, I hurriedly climbed on and wrapped my arms around the large body in front of me. I held on for dear life as Savage twisted the gas, and we practically flew out of there.

We rode for hours, far above the speed limit, until we had to stop for gas at some hole-in-the-wall place near Albuquerque. My ears rang from the wind, and I could barely move my legs to climb off the bike. They wobbled under my weight when I finally managed to stand. It'd been years since I'd been on a motorcycle, at least for any length of time. As soon as I was old enough, I'd distanced myself as much as possible from the MC, not wanting any part of that lifestyle. When Niall and I did anything together, I always drove. So I wasn't exactly used to the constant vibration between my legs. With that and the man I'd had no choice but to hold on to with my breasts pressed against his back, inhaling his scent with each breath, my thighs had stayed clenched the whole time.

"We gotta ride before someone finds you again," Savage said, joining me in front of the shelves of chips inside the shabby store. "Hungry?"

I wasn't sure if I was, my gut all twisted up after everything that had happened, but it had been close to twenty-four hours since I'd eaten before the funeral. Gods. Was that really just yesterday?

Savage must have been starving because he loaded up on beef jerky, chips, and drinks. As soon as he opened the first package of jerky once we were back outside, my stomach rumbled loudly. He handed it over to me, and together we devoured the craptastic junk food. I'd have to eat salads for the next week to make up for it. And then I silently laughed at how unlikely that was.

We rode for a few more hours, and at the next stop, Savage removed his leather jacket and handed it to me.

"Shifter here. I run warm," I reminded him.

"It's dark, we're headed into the mountains, and it's January."

"And what about you?" I eyed his massive body, now clad in only a long-sleeved black shirt and whatever he might have worn underneath it.

"Hellhound here. I self-generate heat."

"Oh. Good point." I took the coat. As soon as I put it on, I wondered if it was a big mistake, because now I would not only be inhaling his scent with every breath, but I was totally enveloped in it.

"Just hope the roads are clear," Savage said before firing up the bike once more.

"Are we almost there yet?" I asked, my body protesting at the thought of getting back on. He looked at me with one of those sharply arched brows raised even higher. "Yes, I'm feeling childish."

"No, we're not." He said no more.

With a resigned sigh, I climbed on.

Savage sped us up the mountains, down the ridges, and up some more. My ears popped at some point. The scenery streaked by us, and even with my supernatural vision, I could only see blurred trees and snow glowing in the darkness. The temperature continued to drop the farther up we climbed, but Savage's body remained toasty warm. I couldn't stop myself from pressing harder against him.

I was comfortable enough—and exhausted enough—that I was about to doze off when something zinged through my body.

"What was that?" I yelped, completely alert now.

"Town's wards," Savage yelled back, the wind devouring his words. He slowed some. "You're safe now."

We rode for another fifteen minutes or so before any kind of town came into sight when we crested a ridge. It was late, but many lights sparkled in the village spread out below us. We were only partly down the ridge, though, when we turned off the road and began to climb again. This road was rougher, but Savage expertly maneuvered the bike around snow and ice patches. We turned off that road onto a gravel driveway that ran through the trees. It opened up, and we came to a stop in front of a log cabin that was way too big to call quaint or cozy. Not a mansion, by any means, but not a one-room rustic shack, either. Savage cut the engine and heaved out a loud grunt as he stood up, signaling for me to climb off before he set the bike on the kickstand.

"Where are we?" I asked as I dismounted.

"Home." He swung his leg over the bike and walked toward the front door.

I hurried after him, but stopped short and gasped when I entered. "Whose home?"

He paused and turned to look at me with the beginnings of a smirk. "Whose the fuck do you think?"

"This is *yours?*"

"Anyone ever tell you not to judge a book by its cover?" He bent over to untie his motorcycle boots.

I gaped, first at him, and then at the house.

The interior was cozier than I thought it would be from the outside, but still open and beautiful. Although the large leather sectional facing the wide, two-story stone fireplace, and the rest of the décor were all very manly, it definitely was not biker bachelor pad style. Still standing in front of the door, I faced a wall of windows looking out on trees and snow, some of the town lights below visible. I couldn't wait to see that view in the morning.

"We're staying here?" I asked.

"Yes." He said it so fast and so firmly, there was obviously no room for argument. Not that I wanted to. But someone did, because when his phone rang on his hip, he answered it with, "I brought her to my place." Pause. "The fuck she's staying at the clubhouse." Another pause as he kicked off his boots, then he turned to glare at me. His voice changed to something almost unrecognizable, almost sweet and way too formal, as he forced a smile. "Ms. Moreno, would you prefer to stay here or at the clubhouse?"

I didn't like it. His tone—it was unnatural and just didn't fit him—or the question.

My nose wrinkled of its own accord. "The clubhouse?"

"She's staying here, Peters," Savage growled, the sound more normal for him, and he ended the call. He leaned against the counter of the island that separated the kitchen from the living room, folded his arms over his chest, and surveyed me. Excitement rippled through my body, but he remained still and quiet, long enough that I began to question everything.

"Um . . . unless it's a bother for me to be here?" I asked, suddenly nervous. He was probably used to having his own space. Or, I considered for the first time, maybe he had an old lady, and I was an unwanted guest. I didn't see any evidence of a woman living here, but maybe she had a more masculine style. Or, with how the whole biker and old lady thing worked, maybe she didn't have a say in the décor at all. "I don't want to intrude."

"I wouldn't have brought you here if I didn't want you here."

"And your . . ." My question lingered on my tongue, because I didn't want to ask—to know. While my brain screamed reminders that he was a biker and I could never be with him, just the thought of him with someone else made me feel sick to my stomach with jealousy. "Uh . . . your old lady?"

He let out the closest thing to a laugh I'd heard from him yet. "No old lady."

I thought I saw another ghost of a smile before he quickly turned and headed for the fridge. He began pulling out the makings of a breakfast. The clock on the stove read 3:06. The witching hour.

"What did you mean by wards?" I asked, while watching him make breakfast.

"What?"

"You said something about the town's wards."

He grunted in acknowledgment. "The town's heavily warded, twenty-five miles out."

When he didn't continue, I had to push for more. "What does that mean?"

He glanced over his shoulder at me, then went back to placing bacon in a pan. "This place is different. It's magically protected by some powerful mages and other supes. You'll see soon enough. Just know you're safe."

I smiled. "Wow. Did you just say more than three sentences in a row? I wasn't sure you were capable."

He snorted. "I'm capable of many things, you'll soon learn."

And the tone in his voice, full of underlying promises, made my already sore thighs squeeze again.

I wasn't sure if he was a really good cook or if I was just that hungry for food that didn't come from a gas station, but I devoured the Southwestern-style breakfast he served. As soon as I swiped the last bit on my plate with a final bite of soft tortilla, exhaustion set in. My belly was full, and my eyelids felt just as heavy.

"I need a shower and a bed," I said on a contented sigh as I leaned back in the barstool.

Just finishing his own meal, Savage looked up at me, still wearing his sunglasses. I wondered if his gaze would hurt me. Usually only immortals and those extremely difficult to kill could tolerate looking into a hellhound's eyes more than two times. Kelpies weren't that strong—but I wasn't a typical kelpie. I wasn't sure how to test it, though, and I'd already been given my first look.

He cleared his throat as he stood, but he still sounded grumbly when he said, "Follow me."

We crossed the living room to a door near the back wall of windows. Through it was a short hallway that opened up to what must have been the master suite, with a bed that appeared larger than a king-size facing another wall of windows. There was a cold stone fireplace in the opposite corner and then more windows that stopped at another doorway. We rounded the bed and entered an impressive bathroom, with a huge bathtub in front of a large picture window. The décor was mostly wood and stone, the flooring a dark gray slate.

Savage threw open a door on the tower of cabinets that reached from floor to ceiling.

"Towels," he grunted, then he pointed at the stone and glass structure in the corner. "Shower."

"I think I figured that one out on my own," I joked. He didn't laugh.

"You're good then?" he asked as he headed back out the door.

I glanced around, about to nod, then something occurred to me.

"Wait." He turned back toward me, cocking his head expectantly. The direct attention caught me a little off guard. "Uh . . . I don't have any, uh, clothes. They were in the RV . . ." I let my voice trail off.

He frowned, then heaved out a breath before heading through another doorway off the bathroom, which appeared to be a closet.

"Here." He left two pieces of fabric on the vanity before striding out.

After closing the door, I leaned against it, closed my eyes, and blew out a breath. The effects of the long ride still hadn't worn off, which was a little disorienting—I was standing still, but felt like the world was still whizzing by. I forced myself to straighten up and peel off my clothes.

The shower was amazing—almost as good as my own at home. Well, my old place that I hadn't been able to live in for nearly a year. So this one felt like heaven, three different heads streaming water on me—one from the front, one from the back, and a rain head from above. Without my own toiletries, I had no choice but to use Savage's. I smiled when I noticed he had both shampoo and conditioner. The man liked to take care of those long, beautiful locks of his. Unfortunately, they weren't Curly Girl–approved, and they'd probably wreak havoc on my hair. I'd have to deal with that tomorrow. There was no way I was sleeping with road-greasy hair.

Once the shower washed away the dirt and grime and the heat relaxed my muscles, I stepped out, dried off, and lifted the two items of clothing he'd left for me. A rather large Metallica T-shirt and a pair of boxer shorts.

"You've got to be kidding me." Holding them out at arm's length, I inspected them carefully. I couldn't exactly go commando, but I wasn't about to wear a man's dirty underwear, either. Peering at them and sniffing from a distance, I realized they were brand new, right out of the package. They had that industrial smell to them, and the inspection sticker was still stuck to the waistband.

With a sigh, I pulled them on, and then the T-shirt. While the underwear smelled new, the shirt most definitely did not. It was clean, but Savage's scent clung to it. I hated how much I liked it. The hem brushed against my mid-thigh, making me feel small, something I rarely ever enjoyed.

I walked into the bedroom to find a fire crackling in the fireplace and Savage on the far side of the bed in nothing but boxers and those sunglasses. We both froze, staring at each other. His body was just as magnificent as I expected it to be. Godlike. Chiseled pecs, a mountain range of ab muscles, massive arms and shoulders, much of his tanned skin covered in ink . . . I swallowed as I broke the eye contact to avert my stare, heat creeping up my neck and cheeks.

As always, I could feel his gaze as a tangible caress even when I couldn't see it. His nostrils flared as it traveled down to my legs, lingering for a moment at the hem of the shirt before coming back up. He grabbed a pillow from the bed, holding it in front of him—but not quick enough for me to miss how the fabric at his crotch had begun to tent.

"I changed—" Savage cleared his throat, but the huskiness didn't leave his voice. "I changed the sheets for you. Just needed to grab a pillow."

My brows pinched together. "Isn't this your bed?"

"Not tonight, it isn't."

"I can take the guest room. I am the guest, after all."

"Don't have one."

I glanced around, bemused. "This big house doesn't have an extra room?"

"That's not what I said. I never have guests, so I don't have a guest room. I'll be on the couch." He turned for the short hallway and strode toward the door.

The bed looked so inviting to my weary body, I could cry. But . . . "You drove for more than twenty-four hours straight while I slept for some of that. This is your house. You take the bed. I can sleep on the couch," I called after him.

"Get in the fucking bed," he snarled before shutting the door behind him, hard enough to make me jump.

As exhausted as I was, sleep evaded me, and not for lack of comfort. The bed was perfectly firm, my head sunk into the mounds of pillows, and the sheets' thread count must have rivaled any luxury hotel, because they felt like silk against my skin. But even though they were clean, they still smelled like Savage, so much that I could taste him in the back of my throat. And that made my breasts tighten and my nipples harden, and every time I shifted to try to get comfortable enough to silence the need, the fabric of his shirt only aroused me more.

I couldn't stop thinking about what it would be like to be with him. He was all man. Big. Rugged. Dangerous. Completely opposite my type, which made him all the more intriguing. Was he into handcuffs, whips, and chains? I imagined his voice and his body were enough to make a girl comply, and imagining that led to envisioning his spectacular naked body towering over mine, his large hands assaulting me in all the right ways as he laid out one-word orders. Just how rough would he be? How badly would it hurt, and how much would I like it?

Though not my usual thing, I gave in to the surprising fantasy and my growing need, slipping my hand under the waistband of his boxers and sliding my finger through my wet folds. I gasped at the sensation and stroked again before finding my clit, circling and rubbing it until it swelled and throbbed. Sliding a finger inside, I brought myself to a quick but silent climax. Unfortunately, it felt hollow, doing little to satisfy the need throbbing through my body—need for something more than I could provide for myself. The need for him.

"Fuck," I heard Savage growl from the living room, and I wondered if he knew what I'd just done. In his bed. In his clothes.

He must have, probably picking up the scent, based on the tone of frustration that filled that one word. I rolled over and smiled as I closed my eyes. My life had spun out of control, but that single groan had sent a surge of power through me, making me feel like I could bring an outlaw named Savage to his knees—in front of my naked body. And that was more satisfying than my self-induced orgasm.

The feeling didn't last long, though. I was just drifting off into dreamland when reality crashed down on me all over again.

What the hell was I doing here? What was happening with my life? And why the hell did Pops have to die?

CHAPTER 4

J awoke to muted light filtering through the floor-to-ceiling windows and someone coming into the room. I quickly ensured all body parts were sufficiently covered before rolling over.

"It's me, love," came Niall's voice before his disfigured frame came into the shadowy room. "Thought you might like your things." He carried in all of my luggage, creating the lumpy silhouette.

"You're okay," I said. The last I'd seen or heard from him was when we left the wreck scene on his bike.

"I am. Not that you seemed too worried—haven't lost any sleep by it, anyway, considering it's two in the afternoon."

My gaze went to the windows, framing the snow-covered trees and gray sky beyond, all I could see from here without sitting up. "I'll have you know that it wasn't any darker than this when I finally fell asleep."

He came closer to the bed, inspecting me, it seemed, as his sapphire gaze roved over me, and his mustache lifted as he smiled. "I figured as much. You got your goods now. You all right, then?"

I pushed myself to sit up against the pillows. "Yeah, I suppose. What happened after we left? Is everyone okay? Were they the same ones who killed Pops?"

He sat on the edge of the bed and frowned as he rubbed and pulled at his beard. "I'm afraid not, from what we could get out of the

29

one faerie, anyway. The one Savage caught. He wasn't very forthcomin', but I'm thinkin' someone back in NOLA tipped 'em off. Only a few knew where we would be, too."

I sucked in a breath. He seemed to be implying that someone in the club gave us up. That was a serious violation of code.

"Pirate and Savage asked me to come to church this afternoon. We got a lot of shit to work out. You okay here?"

Glancing around, I easily nodded.

"Savage okay?"

I shrugged. "He's no Mr. Congeniality, but more of a gentleman than I expected." I lifted my hands and spread them to indicate the bed I sat in. "Case in point."

He patted my leg. "Good, because it's either here or the clubhouse for a while, until we're sure you're indeed safe in this town."

"You know my answer to that. If it's okay with my warden, of course."

He gave a lopsided smile. "This isn't a prison, love. His hellhound's protective instincts have kicked in. If you go to the clubhouse, I'm sure he'd stay there with you. Pirate had to give him a hell of a talkin' to just to get him to leave and come to church."

"Like I said, my warden." I returned his half grin. "I guess we'll both be more comfortable here."

Niall stood. "Just for a few days. When everything settles down and we know for sure their special wards are protecting you, he'll chill, and we can move you to the inn. Nice place, from what I hear."

"And how soon before I can leave? As in, go home?"

He blew out a breath as he stared out the window for a moment, then turned and left without answering me, except to say, "You'll be gettin' a visitor in about an hour for a tattoo. It's her wards protectin' the house and property, so if her arse makes it to the door, you'll know it's her."

"A tattoo?" I called out, but he'd already closed the door.

After hearing him and Savage leave the house, I swung my legs from under the covers and immediately wanted to crawl back into bed. *Good gods, it's cold here!* But the beautiful view drew me to the windows, and I nearly gasped as I looked out. No matter where I gazed, left to right and straight across, were mountains rising high above, their peaks and trees blanketed in snow. I couldn't remember the last time I'd even seen snow. It was a rare occurrence in New Orleans. I'd always wondered what it would be like to be in a winter wonderland, and it looked like I'd be finding out.

A deck ran along the back of Savage's log house, and beyond it was a small lawn that quickly gave way to forest and a sharp descent. In the distance below, the town spread out, some of it visible between the trees. Closer in was a creek and a cemetery—two actually, with a road dividing them. A human probably wouldn't be able to make out the creek, since it was mostly frozen over and covered in fresh snow, or the markers in the cemeteries, but I could. The closer one appeared to be more chaotic, more natural than the other on the far side of the road. This seemed to be the perfect view for a hellhound, protector of not just the living, but also the dead.

A shiver yanked me out of my reverie, and I hurried over to my suitcases to find some warm clothes. I didn't own any winter wear for the mountains, so a soft pink pair of jeans, a camel-colored cashmere sweater, and tan booties with a wedge heel would have to suffice. Just as I'd finished putting on makeup and doing my best to manage my dark curls, feeling more like myself than I had since before Pops died, the doorbell rang—at least, that's what I finally discovered was the cause for what sounded like hounds howling and baying.

A young woman about my age with long light-brown hair trailing out from a slouchy beanie hat, glasses, and a crystal piercing in her nose stood on the other side of the door, a messenger bag slung over her black puffy coat.

"Reyna?" she asked before jutting out her hand. "Addie Beaumont. I've come to register you and ink you up."

I stared at her without extending my own hand, and her brows pinched together.

"They warned you that I was coming, right? I know you're in danger and all, from what I've been told, but I put up the protective wards on this house myself. Trust me—they work. Only certain people

31

can pass through." She tilted her head. "Of course, I guess someone nefarious would make sure they could pass through, huh? Well, I guess you'll just have to trust me." She smiled, still holding her hand out.

I didn't know her from a faerie queen, but she gave off a positive—and powerful—energy. So after another moment's hesitation, I reached out and shook her hand. As soon as we touched, Addie's brown eyes grew wide behind her glasses, and she audibly gasped.

"Whoa," she breathed, still holding on to my hand. "I didn't realize just *how* dangerous of a situation this is. Savage didn't tell me everything. Does he know?"

"Know what?" I asked as I withdrew my hand from hers.

"What you are." She pushed by me, closing the door behind her, but still, her voice dropped to a whisper. "You're a unicorn."

I stepped back. "How did you know?"

She lifted a shoulder in a shrug. "That's my thing, but when I register you, your blood will verify it. Won't it?"

She entered the home as if she was familiar with it and went over to the kitchen island. Shrugging out of her puffy coat, she revealed a hoodie that said *Coexist* but not with the normal religious symbols I'd seen in other, similar designs. The letters seemed to be created by different types of supernatural creatures. Her sleeves were partially pushed up by all the bracelets she wore, and as they swayed with her movement, colorful ink was revealed on her skin underneath.

"Savage said you were a kelpie," she continued as she unloaded some items from her bag onto the granite counter. "I wonder why he lied to me."

"It's not a lie," I said. "I am kelpie."

Her eyes narrowed at me. She didn't believe me.

"I'll find out soon enough." She gestured at one of the barstools. "Have a seat."

"What exactly are we doing?"

Looking up at me, she paused, took a deep breath, and unloaded as though she'd said it a thousand times before. "Our town was specifically founded as a safe haven for the supernatural. A place where all species, including humans, can reside together under secrecy and protection from those who'd like to exploit us. We're able to do this by special protective wards around the town and its outlying areas. We register all supernaturals, residents and visitors alike, so we know who's coming and going—and who's creating problems, especially with the humans. We have two main rules: protect the secret of the supernatural and don't kill humans. Do you have a problem with that?"

I shook my head as I eyed the gun and ink she placed on the counter. "No, but what do tattoos have to do with it?"

"We learned nearly a century ago that it's the best way to ensure we can track the supernaturals, since our ink is impossible to remove. Not even traditional methods of tattoo removal work. Of course, if you leave town, it becomes invisible, and you forget about it, along with everything you know about the town and the people here."

"I'm sorry. I'm still stuck on the 'tracking' part." I really had come to another prison, hadn't I? How long until I could escape?

Addie let out a small laugh. "Yeah, a lot of people get hung up on that part, but it's not what it sounds like. The ink in the tats works with the wards. We only pay attention if there's trouble. If a supernatural energy passes through the wards, everyone in my coven feels a blip. Usually, we ignore it. If it's a threatening energy or trouble ensues after its arrival, though, we know the first place to start looking. Unless you plan on creating problems for us, you have nothing to worry about. We won't even notice you're here."

I gnawed on my lip. "But you would know if someone else, especially the nefarious, as you say, passed through the wards?"

She nodded and smiled. "Sure would. I'm surprised they didn't tell you all this already. I thought it was why they brought you to Havenwood Falls—for the protection we can provide that nobody else can. Especially now that I know what you are."

"They didn't give such a detailed explanation. So the tattoo isn't optional?" It wasn't as though I had anything against ink—in fact, I thought many tattoos were downright beautiful pieces of art—but I'd yet to get one on myself.

"I can make the ink invisible, but no, it's not optional. That's how the magic is infused."

I blew out a breath before finally taking the seat she'd gestured at minutes ago.

"You think about what you want and where, while I do the registry part." She picked up my hand, and with no warning, pricked my finger with a tiny pin. I hadn't even seen her remove it from the package now lying on the countertop. She pressed my finger to a parchment page in a leather-bound book, and writing began to appear. She closed the book before I could read it, and looked at me with a knowing grin. "I was right, of course. About what you are. But so are you. You're a crossbreed?"

"I don't know the history well enough," I admitted. "I'm the only unicorn of our kind—of the kelpie. Every several generations, one of us grows a horn, but whatever the reason for it, it must have been lost somewhere along the way. I happen to be the one this time around."

She studied me, as though trying to ascertain the story from somewhere on my face, then she shrugged. "It just doesn't make sense that Savage didn't say anything about the unicorn part. It's not like I wouldn't find out, and I could have come better prepared."

"Honestly, I'm not sure he knows. I'm just a job—a thing to protect under orders of his president and as a favor to my brother. And, well, now because his instincts have kicked in, and I'm his charge. Nothing more, though. I don't think he really cares what, exactly, I am."

She rolled her eyes. "Hmph, sounds like him. So what do you want and where? Something with a unicorn?" She laughed when I wrinkled my nose and shook my head. "It wouldn't have to be too girly."

"I think Niall would kill me. Even if nobody saw it, it'd still feel like a billboard of what I am."

Her head tilted slightly to the side. "You don't like being a unicorn."

It wasn't a question, and her directness made me squirm.

"I don't like what it means. How it's affected my life," I murmured.

34

"I can imagine it hasn't been easy. Good thing you're here now. Do you have family?"

My throat tightened, and I stared at my hands, breathing deeply as I suffocated the desire to cry. "Just Niall now."

Her hand landed on mine and squeezed. A warm energy passed from her to me. "At least you have him, though, right?"

I lifted my eyes and forced a small smile. "Yeah, thank gods. But he's not blood. My parents, my only blood, sacrificed themselves for me years ago. Pops, who finished raising me, died last week, but his killers had been after me." Blinking rapidly, I sniffed and took another calming breath. "And now . . . I've lost my independence and any kind of freedom to live my life on my terms."

Realizing I'd shared entirely too much, I smacked my mouth closed and looked away.

"So, Niall's the one with the sexy accent?" Addie asked, her tone teasing and lifting the mood. Relief flooded through me. I knew she'd heard the rest, but she'd chosen to focus on the least uncomfortable part of my diatribe. Well, she probably thought it was the least.

My nose wrinkled. "He's like a brother to me. But yes, the one with the Scottish accent. And I guess if he was anyone else, it'd be sexy."

She smiled, and I knew we'd moved past that dark, awkward moment. "Okay, back to business. What tattoo do you want? Maybe a lotus to honor your kelpie?"

My breath catching, I returned her grin with one of my own. The answer came quickly, but not easily or lightly. In fact, I'd been considering a tattoo for a long time. I'd refused for years, because I'd been stubborn and stupid in believing it'd make me too much like the skanks who hung around the MC, screwing whichever brother happened to show interest that day—or could offer the best high. After seeing some incredible artwork on beautiful and professional women, though, including some of the models of my lingerie, I'd started fantasizing about a couple of designs and styles I really liked. I'd just never wanted it badly enough to force myself to choose which one and actually get it done.

"Hold on." I hopped off the stool and rushed for the bedroom. Fishing my laptop out of a suitcase, I opened it as I walked back into the great room, glad to see that the outside, at least, had survived the crash and the trip here. Pressing the power button, I said a prayer to the gods that the inside survived, as well. Thankfully, it had, and within a few moments, I was able to show Addie some of the pictures I'd saved. "Would you be willing to do one of those?"

"Wow, they're amazing. I have a garter one kind of like that." She pointed to the image of a woman's leg with a tattoo of a lacy garter wrapping around her upper thigh, just under her butt, ribbons hanging down the side and front. "Mine has a wand in it, though, like it's a holster." She gave me a toothy grin. "So which one do you want? Here's your lotus." She tapped on the screen.

The water flower really was perfect for my kelpie and my heritage. I described to her the extras I wanted, to honor my parents and Pops —and, in a way, my people. She drew it out on a sketch pad, making adjustments as I talked. When she added in a little extra touch, I realized that it, too, honored those who had sacrificed their lives for me. A little acknowledgment to show that they hadn't died in vain.

"It's unbelievably perfect. You're sure you don't mind?" I asked.

She waved her hand, dismissing my concern. "I've done tattoos on pretty much all body parts, both male and female. This is nothing. Just be ready, because the next day or so is going to be fucking miserable."

"I hadn't thought of that." I shrugged. "Well, it's not like I can go anywhere in public anyway for a while. I'll just be hanging out at the house, and if Savage sees . . . well, I'm not sure if I'd mind that anyway." I clapped my hand over my mouth, wishing I could take that back. Now it was Addie's turn to wrinkle her nose. "You don't like him?"

Her face took on a greenish tint, and she looked like she was trying to suppress a shudder. "Not in that way. But hey, each to her own. I like you, and maybe you'd be good for him. I'm just not sure I can picture you two together."

"Honestly, neither can I."

"But?" This girl was way too intuitive. That's a witch for you.

"But . . . I can't *stop* picturing it either." *Damn it, Rey. Shut the hell up already.* I covered my mouth again, unsure of where all this candidness was coming from. It so wasn't like me. I blamed the witch. She was too easy to talk to.

Once again showing that she could easily read me—or maybe for her own reasons—she quickly changed the subject. "We should probably go somewhere more private than out here. In case he comes home—and possibly not alone."

I glanced around, unfamiliar with most of the house. "Will the bed be okay?"

"Not ideal, but it'll work." She gathered her tools and followed me into Savage's bedroom. "Or that chaise longue would be better."

She pointed across the room. I hadn't even noticed it in the corner, wedged between the fireplace and the windows. I'd been too enamored with the view outside, I supposed.

While Addie hunted for outlets and moved the long chair for better lighting and accessibility, I turned my back and removed the necessary clothing before lying on the chaise, shyly covering myself with my hands as much as I could.

Addie lifted a brow when she saw me. "Please don't feel like you need to be modest for my sake. Like I said, I've seen a lot—and rarely as nice as this."

Heat crept up my neck and cheeks, and I held my position for a while as she began, but at some point, the discomfort of my arms and the increased ease of being with this woman I'd just met an hour ago won out. My hands fell away, and I sighed as blood flowed back into them.

"You know, you can have that freedom and independence you want here in Havenwood Falls," Addie said as she worked.

I stared outside at the scene of snow and evergreens, catching the pounce of a small fox hunting for food, the snow spraying up around him as his face plunged into the white stuff. "Here? In the middle of nowhere?"

"Well, there are benefits to being in the middle of nowhere, especially this place." She continued on for a while, selling her little town as the best town anywhere on earth, as though she hoped I'd buy a house tomorrow and bring all my tax dollars. I could hear the sincerity in her tone, though—she really believed this *was* the best town.

"I don't think this place is exactly my style. I'm a city girl. But even if you're right, I doubt Niall and the hellhounds will let me out of this prison for a while."

"I think you'll be surprised. They called me over here immediately for a reason, and not only because it's town law for you to be registered in the first forty-eight hours. The MC isn't exactly known for abiding by the law, you know, but Savage and Liam know what I can do for you, and they'll convince Niall."

"Liam?"

"The other hellhound. President of SIN?"

"You mean Pirate?"

"Ah." She nodded. "I guess that's how you'd know him, by his road name. He's always been Liam Peters to me."

"So what *are* you doing for me, Addie?" I asked.

She paused and looked up at me with that winning smile. "Like I said, giving you your freedom."

Another hour passed before Addie started doing the cleanup work, gingerly wiping at me with a cloth. I could see pink tinge her cheeks while heat flooded mine at her touch. Then she placed her hand over the artwork and closed her eyes. Her lips moved with some kind of utterance, and at the same time, a warm energy flowed into me, twisting and curling through the fresh ink.

"Done," she announced. "You are not only registered with the wards, but I gave it a little something extra to help keep you protected. Your freedom, so to speak. As well as something for you and Savage. It could make life easier if you'll be staying here at his house." She explained further as she stood and arched her back in a stretch. "Well, are you going to go check it out?"

Forgetting all modesty, I scrambled to my feet and hurried to the bathroom. My jaw dropped when I saw myself in the mirror. I was so impressed with the artwork and the overall effect, I didn't even cover myself when Addie came in.

"Do you like it?" she asked.

"I, uh, flipping *love* it!"

She laughed. "You really have a great rack, you know, but now it's just sexy as fuck. And I don't even like girls."

My turn to laugh as I twisted and turned to study the design from all angles. A large lotus covered my sternum, the tip of the top petal twisting into a unicorn horn that rose up between my breasts and ended with a fleur de lis. Scalloped lace and chains with dangling charms arced underneath each breast, framing them perfectly, the longest piece hanging down the center to end a couple of inches above my navel. I couldn't stop staring at it, which wasn't really like me. And I couldn't stop thinking about Savage staring at it—and tracing the lines with his fingers . . . his tongue—which seriously wasn't like me.

What the hell was going on with me? Was it this place—or that man—making me so crazy?

At least there was one thought to hang on to: I didn't plan for either to be lasting in my life.

CHAPTER 5

*N*ot that Addie hadn't done a terrific job of selling Havenwood Falls to me. And the scene from Savage's windows was picture-postcard perfect. It just wasn't New Orleans. It wasn't home.

I loved to travel, though I rarely ever got to. This was the kind of place I'd love to visit and spend a little time exploring. And that's all I'd be doing—visiting, exploring, then leaving.

If Niall and the hellhound ever let me.

Speaking of, they walked in just as Addie was leaving. Niall handed me a box with a new phone in it.

"Accounts have already been set up so they can't be traced, so don't go connecting to your old ones," he warned. "My number is in there, and so is Savage's. Both on autodial. Now, you wanna go shopping?"

"Shopping?" I echoed with surprise.

"You need some winter clothes, love. At least boots and a coat, because what you have on—you'll freeze your arse off here." He eyed my outfit. "Unless you plan on staying in the house all the time?"

I blinked, still in shock. I actually had planned on staying in the house because I didn't think they'd let me go anywhere. "It's safe?"

"Addie inked you, eh?" Niall scanned me again, looking for my tattoo. "You're not goin' to show me?"

"Uh, that's a big negative," I said, a little too quickly. He picked up on my meaning, and so, apparently, did Savage, because he suddenly looked up from the mail in his hand with interest. Why did that cause tingles to run along my skin?

"My little Rey got a little crazy, eh?" Niall grinned, and I denied him an answer.

We piled into the only vehicle in the garage that wasn't a motorcycle—a shiny black Cadillac SUV. The rough biker continued to surprise me. He drove us into town with Niall in the front passenger seat. I looked out the back window as we descended the mountain and turned onto a main road that took us right into downtown Havenwood Falls. We passed a high school on the left, and on the right, a burger joint with a neon sign reading *Burger Bar* that looked like it was stuck in the fifties. A shopping plaza sprawled behind it. Looking down the side streets as we passed, the residences appeared to be an eclectic mixture of everything from old Victorians to modern cement-and-glass structures, with plenty of bungalows and log cabins sprinkled in. Ski lifts climbed up the mountain to our right with several cleared trails and slopes coming back down.

Cute town, just as Addie had made it out to be.

When we rolled in to what was obviously the town's central business district, I sat up a little straighter. As though giving a grand, though silent, tour, Savage drove all the way around the square, past quaint little stores and coffee shops. The area reminded me of a small version of Jackson Square Park back home, except where St. Louis Cathedral sat in New Orleans was a building with a clock tower and *City Hall* embossed into one of the stones. The center square was a park-like setting with a fountain in the center and even a gazebo decorated with twinkle lights. Twilight was quickly descending, so everything was lit up, and talk about picture-postcard perfect. It was like a town straight out of the movies—one of those cheesy Hallmark holiday ones, considering everything was blanketed in fresh snow. Those movies may or may not have been a guilty pleasure over the holidays.

Savage parked in front of a place called Backwoods Sport & Ski.

Seriously? Did I look like the type for this place? When we walked in, the guys flanking me, everyone turned to look at us, then scattered. Except for a young girl who stayed at the cash register, eyeing us. Her nametag said Willa. She smelled like a wolf.

"Let me guess, you need bike gear?" she asked as she came out from behind the counter, her gaze bouncing to the bikers right behind me before landing back on my face.

"Um, no." I glanced over at their women's clothing section, which was definitely not what I was accustomed to—the small selection or the styles. "I guess just a coat and boots."

"Cross country or downhill?" she asked.

"Not ski boots," Savage rumbled. "Walking."

She seemed to shrink a little at his gruff voice, and I wished I could elbow him in the ribs. Up until that moment, she'd given off a more confident air than normal for her age—the air of a leader. He didn't need to be knocking her down. Being a teenage girl was hard enough, especially in the supe world.

"Well, we have, uh, some good hiking boots." She led me over to the shoe section, and eventually I found a pair of boots that would keep my feet warm and weren't completely hideous. In fact, they were somewhat fashionable—if this look was your thing. It wasn't mine.

We then looked at coats, hoodies, pants, and socks. Niall and Savage never strayed more than five feet from me, scaring off anyone who tried to come close simply by their overbearing presence. Except for Willa, bless her heart. She hung right in there, helping me find the cutest things they had to offer. I left with a bag of clothes I'd never be seen in again once I left town, but I threw the coat on right away and sighed from its warmth.

"Did you lose your love for shopping?" asked Niall, who was used to me leaving stores with multiple bags.

"Not exactly my kind of place."

"Ah. Well, you can do your online thing then. You'll need more than what you have there."

I nodded, but wasn't too worried about it. I had enough to get by for a few days of lounging around the house and maybe taking a walk in the woods. And surely they had washing machines in this town.

"Try Callie's," Savage said, lifting his bearded chin toward the line of buildings perpendicular from the one where we were parked. "Looks like she's still open. Might not be much longer."

Niall put my bag in the SUV, then we made our way over there, passing by a jewelry store on the corner before crossing the street diagonally. Then we passed a bar with old-fashioned swinging doors marked *Haven Saloon*, a bookstore called Shelf Indulgence with an elaborate wintry display in the window, and a coffee shop with a sign that said *Coffee Haven*, which was closed for the day.

"You got five minutes, and then I'm closing," a voice called out when we entered the store marked *Callie's Consignments*.

It was an eclectic sort of place, expansive and filled with a variety of vintage-looking clothes. Still not my style, but I was drawn in anyway by all the colors and textures. Someone here had an obvious talent for merchandising and an eye for design. I looked up a staircase to a second floor, catching glimpses of old but stylish furniture beyond the railings.

"I'm serious. I'm already here later than I'd planned." The owner of the sassy voice appeared from behind a display of dresses, her hazel eyes going wide when she looked over my shoulder, where the two burly men in their leather cuts stood. "Oh, uh, well." She broke her gaze from them to land on me and stuck out a hand while plastering on a fake smile. "Callie Montgomery. Sorry. I, uh, just wasn't expecting . . . customers."

She meant customers like us. Well, like the two outlaws who refused to leave my side.

I shook her hand, showing that I was civil, even if they weren't. "Reyna. And we won't stay. I love your store, so I had to sneak a peek, but I can come back another time."

She waved an arm, her many bracelets clinking together as she did, reminding me of Addie. While both gave off a hippie-like aura, the witchy tattooist's style was a little different than this girl's. Although I'd only met her once, I sensed that Addie's all-black wardrobe was common for her, dressed up only with jewelry, all of the metaphysical kind. This woman was more colorful and feminine, dressed in a gauzy top and long skirt, decorated with colorful scarves and jewelry.

She flipped her hand in the air. "You're here. I'm here. You may as well look around. Anything you're looking for in particular?" Her gaze scanned over my puffy ski jacket and the rest of my much nicer outfit. "Maybe a coat?"

I chuckled. "It's not that ugly, is it?"

Callie cringed. "Well . . . it just doesn't seem like you. Come. Follow me."

I didn't have the heart to tell her that there was probably nothing here that was me, either. Instead, I followed her toward the back of the store, Savage and Niall on my heels, to a rack of leather coats. She flipped through them, then pulled a dark brown one off and displayed it with a swoosh of her hand. I stared, no words forming.

"Right?" she said with a twinkle in her eyes. "Feel it."

As though compelled, my hand reached out and petted the soft leather. "Wow."

"Go on. Try it on." She thrust it into my hand.

The skin under my breasts was already sore, but I gritted my teeth as I shrugged off the ski jacket and pulled this one on. Callie led me over to a three-way mirror.

"It's meant to be yours!" she declared. "I don't think it would fit anyone more perfectly."

I glanced at her reflection, but didn't see a hint of cruelty or teasing in her expression or hear it in her voice. I didn't exactly have an off-the-rack body type. Rarely did anything fit me perfectly unless it had been custom made for me—the whole reason I went into clothing design myself. But this wasn't off the rack. It was vintage and unique, the cut just right to emphasize my breasts and diminish my waist while flaring out over my round hips and ass. The hem hit my knees, giving me plenty of butt protection from the cold.

"I have some boots that came in with it. They're not exactly for hiking or anything, but a little more practical than those heels, when it gets icy." She took my hand and pulled me over to the shoe section, picking out a pair of knee-high, low-heeled boots. "Size ten?"

My size, but again, I hesitated, knowing my calves were usually too large for standard-sized tall boots. But again, I was surprised. They fit just as well as the coat did, like they were made for me. Shrugging off the coat, I gave myself another look in the mirror for a better look and caught Savage's reflection. Though his eyes were forever hidden by the shades, I again felt the weight of his gaze on me. I felt my eyes lock with his, holding for a long moment as his tongue swiped over his lips. I mirrored the gesture, and he made that growly rumbling sound before turning away. There was something feral yet empowering about his response. I smiled to myself, butterflies taking off in my belly.

"Feel free to look around," Callie offered. "Between us, I wasn't really in a huge hurry to leave anyway, now that I know you're not one of the broke-ass teens who only come to try on every item on the rack while giggling over boys, only to leave empty-handed."

She left me alone. Well, not really alone. I tried to browse the shop —there was so much to see, a surprise around every corner—but the guys continued hovering, making it difficult to relax. One other woman entered the store, looked at the three of us, and turned right back around before Callie could even welcome her. Between that and my clothing rubbing against my freshly inked skin, I'd had enough. I was already headed for the counter when the door chimed again.

"Savage!" a familiar voice barked out. We all looked at Addie standing there, her brow raised high into her beanie hat and her hands on her hips. "Outside. Now."

"Oh, shit," Callie muttered with a chuckle.

To my surprise, Savage gave a soundless nod to Niall, then obediently strode outside, his booted steps heavy on the carpeted floor.

"She's about the only person who could get away with that," Callie whispered as I placed my items on the counter to make my purchase.

"Are they . . . ?" I didn't know how to finish my thought, not sure what I was asking or what I wanted to know.

"Their history is . . . weird. But that's all I'm saying." Callie quickly busied herself by ringing up my two items.

Niall came up next to me, pulling his wallet out, since I couldn't use any of my cards. While he and Callie handled the transaction, I watched out the window as Addie seemed to be giving Savage a piece of her mind. She did all the talking, throwing her arms up animatedly, gesturing toward the store—toward me, no doubt—more than once. What the hell? She'd acted like she wanted nothing to do with him, but now seemed to be . . . jealous? I wasn't sure if that was the right word, but she was definitely angry about something. Even with my supernatural hearing, I couldn't catch any of their words, and I wondered if she'd used a muffling spell. After another moment, she stomped off, leaving Savage outside, standing in front of the door. His back was to us, so I couldn't read his expression.

"You didn't need to rush for me," he said gruffly when we exited the store.

"Uh, I was done in there," I said, confused by his tone and meaning.

"Where now, then? All the shops will be closing soon."

"Actually, I'm good." My stomach rumbled at that moment. "Well, I'm starving. I haven't eaten all day. But I've had enough shopping."

I wasn't sure there were too many more places to go anyway, and what was the fun in discovering the whole town within a couple of hours?

"We'll take Napoli's home," Savage said, then waved me in the direction of the car. "This way."

This time, as we walked toward the vehicle, Savage seemed to be keeping a lot more space between us. He wasn't breathing down my back like he had been earlier. I hadn't minded too much, because he was warm, and I wasn't used to these freezing temperatures that were plummeting even more now that night had fallen. Addie must have really gotten to him. I liked her and didn't want to create an enemy—especially after seeing the man named Savage, the man I'd witnessed nearly kill a fae without a bat of an eye, submit to her so easily. So I'd keep my distance, too.

Savage must have remotely started the car, because it was nice and toasty when I slid into the back seat. He and Niall exchanged a few words before he sauntered off farther down the block and rounded the corner. After taking off his cut, Niall climbed into the front seat.

"You sure you'll be all right with him tonight?" he asked, turning in his seat to face me. "I need to get back to the clubhouse and see if they were able to find out anything. They got this guy, Axle, who's magic on the dark web. Should be able to find any intel on our attackers."

I shrugged. "I have a feeling I'll be entertaining myself, but I'm sure I'll be fine."

"Good. I'll be able to breathe easier once I know we can take care of those guys. With your trail cold, you should be good for a while."

"And when can I go home?"

Niall didn't answer, his gaze dropping.

"Niall?" I pressed.

He sighed and looked out the window, toward the lit-up ski slopes. "Why don't you just enjoy yourself, love? This place has a lot to offer."

I snorted. "You've been here one day, and you already sound like Addie."

"Turns out, I've been here before. I'd forgotten about it, after I left, but my memories are coming back now. That's how their wards work. I'd been trying to get Pops to move you here a while ago, but you refused to leave New Orleans." He stopped there, but I inferred the rest. Staying in NOLA had gotten Pops killed.

I turned to look out the window myself, not wanting to think about that, and was glad to see Savage striding down the sidewalk with two big bags in his hands. When he opened the back door and set them on the floor, my mouth immediately watered at the fragrances of cheese, tomatoes, and garlic.

We left the town square area by a different street than we'd entered, passing by a majestic Victorian structure with a wooden sign in the lawn that said Whisper Falls Inn. A couple of blocks down, we entered a sort of industrial area with warehouses. We pulled into a parking lot between one such warehouse and a brick building with the SIN logo over the door. Niall said his goodbyes and slid out, leaving me in the back seat and Savage in the front.

"Hey! What the hell are you doing?" Savage growled when I opened my door. He jumped out of the car as I slid out and rushed over to my side.

"You don't exactly have the right demeanor to be a chauffeur," I said as I reached for the handle of the front passenger door. With a harsh exhale that bloomed out in a fog, he grabbed it first and opened the door for me.

We rode in silence for several minutes, leaving the main part of town behind and passing by the high school again, this time on the right.

"How does it all work—the wards and everything?" I asked, trying to strike up a conversation. "I understand that the magic-infused ink works with them, but Niall said he's been here before but had forgotten about it because of the wards."

"Visitors lose their memories as soon as they pass through them. Remember when you felt us enter the wards?"

I nodded. "So what? Your memories get wiped when you leave?"

"Right away for visitors. Residents get a lunar cycle, but we can't talk about Havenwood Falls or the people here. The magic fucks with us, tying up our tongues or making us forget what we were saying if we try to share too much."

I watched the snowy night pass by. "So as soon as I leave, I'll forget all about this place and everyone I've met."

He was quiet for a long moment. "Yeah, you will."

We drove the rest of the way in more silence. Not until we were seated at the kitchen island with a spread of pasta and bread did we talk again.

"I wasn't sure what you like," Savage said, "so I got a variety. Assuming you're not one of those salad-only girls."

I gave him a sideways glance. Did I look like a salads-only girl? Not that it mattered. Even if I was, I was just big-boned and would never be considered petite. Perhaps because I was part horse.

"I think I need to try everything." Smiling, I doled out a spoonful of chicken alfredo, another of lasagna, and grabbed one each of garlic knots and fried mozzarella. "So I'm still trying to understand. How do you get supplies and inventory for the stores if nobody knows where this town is to deliver to?"

He swallowed the big bite of pasta he'd already taken. "CDI takes care of all the deliveries in and shipments out. Cerberus Delivery, Inc. —my and Liam's business. Our guys drive and escort the trucks. It's the legit side of the club."

"Legit?" I asked with a raised brow and a smirk.

He shrugged. "As close to legit as we get."

"So there's no smuggling or anything going on . . ."

"You're here, aren't you?" And though I could barely see his eyes behind the darkly tinted glasses, I swore he winked at me.

"What else do you smuggle? What other kinds of jobs do you take?"

He stood and carried his plate to the sink. "Sweetheart, you're much more than a job."

He said no more, avoiding my question as he dropped his plate and fork into the dishwasher.

"I'm going out to get some wood," were his only other words before he disappeared down the hall that led to the part of the house I hadn't been shown yet.

I cleaned my own dishes and put the leftovers in the refrigerator, but Savage hadn't returned, so I slipped into the bedroom, planning to retire for the night. I needed to remove my bra, the friction against my tattoo driving me insane. Shutting the door behind me, I stripped off my top and bra, dropping them on my suitcase and sighing with relief as I walked into the bathroom. My own image in the mirror stopped me, the dark ink on my golden brown skin looking even prettier than it had earlier, now that it was no longer red and raised. I could see where my bra had been bothering it, but my own healing properties had taken away the worst of the sting already. Opening the little jar of salve Addie had left on the bathroom counter for me, I rubbed it on.

"Oh, gods . . . yes," I moaned, the ointment immediately relieving the irritation—and realizing a moment too late that the little sound I'd heard was a soft knock on the bedroom door. Ointment in one palm and my other hand cupping under my bare breast, I turned at the movement in the corner of my eye to find Savage standing in the bedroom staring at me, the logs in his arms rolling to the floor with a loud clatter.

We both stood frozen, just staring at each other for a long moment. Long enough for my boobs to tighten and my nipples to harden—and for him to shift his hips as a very noticeable bulge twitched in his jeans.

"I thought you meant yes as in *enter*," he accused, his voice thick and his gaze still weighing heavy on my chest.

Coming to my senses, I spun around and grabbed a towel to cover myself since my shirt was on the other side of the bed—past Savage.

"Uh, yeah, um, completely my fault," I stammered. Sufficiently covered, I turned back around to find him picking up the wood.

"I thought you'd want a fire. And I need workout clothes."

"Okay." I still stood just inside the bathroom like a deer in headlights. My breasts swelled painfully under my arm as he quickly built the fire, an obvious expert at it. Then he stood and moved to the bathroom door. "What are you doing?" I squeaked.

"My closet is through there." He gestured, though I already knew that.

"Oh, uh, right." My brain focused on trying to escape the bathroom and nothing else, I moved forward instead of backward and out of his way, and at the same time, he stepped in. We bumped into each other, and my towel shifted. His arm brushed across my exposed breast, and we both froze again. That one soft touch sent my heart racing even faster than it had been and made my stomach flip over. Wet need pooled between my legs at the same time he inhaled deeply.

"Fuck, woman, you're going to kill me," he growled without looking over at me. Then he murmured so quietly, he probably didn't think I'd hear, "The things I want to do to you . . ."

My breath caught.

"Are you able to?" I asked, sudden boldness coming from somewhere unknown.

He looked over his shoulder, his brows drawn together. "What the fuck does that mean?"

"Well, are you . . . free?"

"I don't have a woman, if that's what you mean."

I nodded, and we continued to stare at each other.

"So . . . how about we just get the fuck part over with?" I blurted, my brain apparently having gone into shutdown mode.

A low rumble sounded deep in his throat, before he turned his whole body toward me and advanced until I was pressed up against the door jamb. His hands cupped the sides of my face as he came in even closer, my arm between us, trying to hold the towel somewhat in place. I could feel his eyes piercing into mine.

"Is that what you really want?" he growled.

I stared up at him. "Don't you?"

He shifted his hips forward, offering me his answer by grinding his erection against my belly. I let go of the towel to give him mine.

CHAPTER 6

*H*e leaned in, his lips parting, but first, I stopped him by reaching up for the sunglasses.

"You can't," he snarled.

"It's okay. I'm safe from your death glare."

I slid the sunglasses off and stared up into beautiful hazel eyes framed with long dark lashes. They were filled with apprehension at first, but then a hunger I'd never seen in a man's eyes before—at least, not while looking at me. He wanted me at least as badly as I wanted him. In fact, maybe even more, the way his whole body vibrated as we looked into each other's eyes, a soft orange glowing in the depths of his. Okay, safe might not have been the best word, but his gaze wasn't going to actually kill me. Send me into cardiac arrest, maybe, from that lascivious way he watched me, but not make me drop dead.

"Fuck," he muttered, his lids dropping. "This is a bad idea."

"It is."

He nodded, opening his eyes again, staring right into mine. "I don't think I can stop, though."

"Then don't." I grasped his face like he had mine and pulled him to me, our mouths crashing together.

Our lips moved as though we'd both been starving for this, our tongues immediately finding each other as if they were long lost mates. He tasted like he smelled—of oak and fire and whiskey. His beard rubbed roughly against my skin, the abrasion turning me on even more. His hands slid down my shoulders, finding my breasts and squeezing. I groaned, and then gasped when he pinched and rolled my nipples. Then he palmed his way down my sides, his fingers lightly brushing over my ribs, careful to avoid the tattoo. Sliding his hands to my ass, he lifted me up, and I wrapped my legs around him, grinding against his bulge as he carried me into the bedroom. He groaned into my mouth before dropping me to the bed.

Standing over me, he pulled his shirt off, exposing the perfection of his torso I'd seen last night. The man could seriously play a god in a movie—Adonis had nothing on him, was barely more than a boy compared to Savage. His gaze traveled to my breasts as his hands undid his buckle. Watching him, I played with my nipples as my tongue darted over my lips.

He groaned and then commanded, "Take your fucking clothes off, woman."

"You take them off," I countered.

He lifted one of those sharp brows, and I wondered if anyone had ever challenged him in this way before. Part of me wanted to obey everything he said as long as it meant his cock would be inside me soon, but another part couldn't help but do the opposite.

In one quick motion, he grabbed me at the waist and lifted me to stand on the bed in front of him. Even as tall as I was, I still barely looked down at him.

"I said to take your fucking clothes off." His hand jerked at my waistband, somehow undoing the button and the zipper without ripping a single thread.

I grabbed his hands and placed them on my hips, sliding them underneath the straps of my panties. "And I said for you to do it."

Together we pushed my jeans and panties down at once, and I stepped out of them at the same time he stepped out of his. I kicked mine off to the side, off the bed. His gaze raked over me, a certain carnality in it that made my legs weak. Well, that and his enormous cock standing tall and thick.

"God damn, you're fucking gorgeous."

"So are you," I breathed as his mouth clamped onto one of my breasts, drawing it in as his hand played with the other. My fingers slid into his long locks, grasping his head as my back arched, thrusting my breast farther into his mouth. His tongue circled the hard pebble of my nipple, then his teeth grazed over it, biting just hard enough to feel good.

He pulled away too soon, panting, his breath hot on my already burning skin.

"Turn around," he ordered.

I cocked a brow, but then made the decision to obey, if for no other reason, to see where it would go. Besides, I was too wet and needy to argue. I turned on the bed and looked over my shoulder. His hand lifted, sweeping my curls to the side. He grasped my shoulder while his other hand lightly brushed down my spine, sending chills over my skin. As his fingers reached the small of my back, the hand on my shoulder pushed me forward.

"On your hands and knees," he said, his voice mesmerizing, authoritative, giving me no choice but to obey.

I knew exactly the view in front of him now, and just the thought of it made my core clench. I should have felt embarrassed, my ass and pussy on full display for him, but I didn't. All of my inhibitions I'd always carried into my few previous sexual encounters suddenly fell away. He did that to me. I'd known him for two whole days, but he already made me feel safer and more comfortable than anyone I'd ever dated.

"Fucking gorgeous," he muttered again, and maybe that was why. He appreciated my body, soft, luscious curves and all, where most men were intimidated or worse—rudely critical.

He leaned over, hovering over me so his cock rubbed against my ass as his lips landed lightly on the nape of my neck. One hand slid around, cupping my breast, his mouth slowly making its way down my spine. His tongue swirled along my skin. His fingers squeezed and tweaked. Goose bumps rose over my flesh. He took his time, as though appraising with his lips and tongue every inch of my back. My inner beast awakened inside me.

Releasing my shoulder, he grabbed my ass cheek as his mouth lowered. His tongue circled over a dimple before moving to my other cheek. His hand abandoned my breast, traveling down until his finger slid between my folds, quickly finding my already swollen clit. He kissed and sucked at the flesh of my ass as he worked my clit, stroking and rolling, building me quickly to an orgasm.

Then he bit my ass. Hard.

I cried out, not in pain but in ecstasy. His tongue swirled over it, as though to soothe the pain, taking me even closer to the edge. His fingers still stroking, circling, and pinching my clit, his other hand pushed my shoulders down so my breasts pressed into the bed and my ass lifted higher in the air. Then his fingers left me, and I whimpered as he knelt behind me. His hands slid between my legs, pushing them further apart, then grabbed my ass again, separating my cheeks. He groaned, and I looked over my shoulder to see him appraising me once again. My kelpie shuddered and my thighs trembled as his tongue slid out, over his lips. Then he finally leaned forward, his mouth taking over where his fingers had left off.

He was an expert, his tongue flattening into my folds and licking once . . . twice . . . three times. His thumbs opened me wider, and his tongue circled and pressed against my clit, teasing it until I was whimpering and moaning. Then it dove inside my opening, making me cry out as I rocked against him. One thumb brushed over my puckered hole, then gave a slight pressure, almost entering.

"Oh, fuck," I screamed, bucking against his face.

"Come for me," he ordered, his breath hot on my sensitive sex, but he didn't have to. I was already there, crying out his name as his tongue swept in again.

Just as I peaked, he smacked my ass right where he'd bitten it before, and I came completely unglued. The world shattered around me, everything diminishing to only the physical sensations of my orgasm. It came in wave after wave, my stomach dropping like it does on a roller coaster, time after time after time. And I realized I'd never truly orgasmed before—not like this anyway.

At some point while I was falling apart, he'd managed to put on a condom, because I'd barely finished when his cock was pressed against my opening.

"Hang on, sweetheart." He grabbed my hips and thrust inside me, making me scream again. He stretched me wide, then filled me thoroughly and perfectly. My core clenched around him.

I expected sex to be rough with him. That might have been what had me so intrigued, because I'd never experienced what I'd imagined it would be like with him. And he didn't disappoint. Far from it. His cock was huge, proportionate to his body, and my pussy loved every swollen, hard inch of it. My ass loved how he slammed against it with each thrust in, and how his thumb again pressed against the most sacred area that I'd never understood as an erogenous zone until now as it barely stretched in a slightly painful but tantalizing way. My muscles squeezed around him as he pulled outward, only to drive into me again. I rocked fast and hard against him, fucking him as fiercely as he fucked me. Like I'd never fucked before.

He broke me apart nine ways to Sunday, feeding the need that had been building in me for months. No, years. Since the first time sex had even been a thought for me. This was what I'd been starving for all this time.

He made me feel like his Athena—like his goddess. A sex goddess who knew how to give and receive pleasure that went way beyond this world. I felt powerful . . . empowered. Especially as his rhythm increased, and I felt him losing control.

"Fuck, *yes*," he groaned as he pounded into me. I could feel him on the verge of climaxing, bringing me to yet another one myself, squeezing and thrusting my ass against him, twisting and rolling my hips until he shouted with his release at the same time mine came. We froze, every single muscle clenched as we rode the waves of ecstasy out together.

Then we both collapsed on the bed, me face down, him on top of me, our breaths coming fast and hard. I was sore all over, but never ever had I been so sated as I was at that moment.

Once our bodies stopped quaking with aftershocks, he rolled off me and got up to clean off. On legs like jelly, I managed to follow him into the bathroom to do the same, and when he turned to look at me, his gaze traveling up and down my body, I suddenly felt very shy and wished I had something to cover up with. My arms moved in, kind of doing the best they could. He frowned.

"That might have been the best bad idea I've ever had," he said, turning around. He walked over to the shower, his back muscles rippling and his perfectly round ass looking as though it were made of steel.

"I think that was my bad idea," I corrected.

"Well, I have another one." He tilted his head, inviting me in.

We fucked again in the shower, my back against the wall and my legs around his hips. I'd never been able to do that with a man before —none had been able to hold me up in that position, but Savage acted as though I weighed no more than a buck at the most. This time was slower and gentler, not as rough as before, but I'd been right when I saw him for the first time: He was a savage in bed. And my body—and my inner beast—couldn't get enough.

"THIS IS SEXY AS FUCK." Savage's finger trailed over my tattoo the next morning as we lay in bed—well, afternoon. Our hours were all messed up after that long drive, and we'd been up until sunrise again, though this time tossing and turning in a completely different way.

"That's what Addie said." Regret filled me as soon as the words popped out of my mouth.

Savage groaned and rolled onto his back. "Why the fuck did you have to say her name? You ruined my moment."

I grimaced. "Sorry. I, uh, well . . . I don't exactly know what the deal is with you two, but there's something. Just know that I don't plan on coming in between you and anyone. This . . . this was just two consenting adults having fun. Right?"

He continued staring at the ceiling, his only response a grunt.

"I mean, we're complete opposites. Last night was amazing, and I wouldn't mind doing it again. But you're you and I'm me, and I will never be anyone's old lady. And I know that's your life and your thing. So this is just what it is—a good time." I didn't know what was wrong with me. I couldn't shut the hell up. The thoughts had been going through my head since the moment I'd woken up—probably even while I'd slept. I had this desperate need for him to know that I didn't expect anything from him—and that I didn't want him to expect anything from me.

"Do you even know what it means to be an old lady?" he asked.

"I practically grew up in the club life. Yes, I know. You give up your life for the club. You become a possession, and will never be a partner. Everything is about the club, and you come after that."

He rolled onto his side to look at me, his gaze traveling over my naked body. Feeling incredibly self-conscious, I pulled the sheet up over my breasts.

"Don't fucking do that," he snarled, yanking it back down.

"See? You're already ordering me around."

He scowled. "I just want to look at you. You're too fucking beautiful to cover up." My whole body might have flushed, and it took everything I had not to cover it up again as his eyes again raked over me. "Being an old lady means you're protected for your whole life, even if your old man dies. It means nobody in the club can fuck with you, and anybody outside of the club who fucks with you fucks with the whole club. You will always have what you need and be taken care of. You're not a possession. You're family."

"But the club always comes first," I countered.

"You're part of the club."

"Not really."

"Well, you don't get to vote," he conceded.

"You don't get to go to church at all," I pointed out. "You know nothing about the club's business—your old man can't share anything with you—but you must abide by all the rules anyway and accept their decisions, regardless of how they affect you. You have no say, but you must meet their demands. That sounds like they own you. That makes you a possession."

"Family," he repeated.

"Which is still secondary to the club. If you had to choose between your old lady and your club, you'd have to choose the club."

He frowned again. "It's not like that."

"It's not?" I lifted a brow.

"No. It doesn't have to be an either-or."

I studied him like he'd been studying me. "Do you want an old lady, Savage? Have you ever had one?"

He stared at me for a long moment, our gazes locked. "How can you look in my eyes? You should be dead by now."

I laughed at his pathetic change of subject. "The witch who shall not be named thought it would help if she gave my ink a little extra magic. She said it wouldn't work on just anyone, not even most supes. But I'm not just anyone and not like most supes, and apparently it worked. Since, you know, I'm not dead by now. Do you have a problem with it?"

He broke our hold and rolled away, getting out of bed. "It's a little unnerving. I'm not used to it."

I smiled to myself. Big badass biker boy felt vulnerable.

AFTER EATING leftover pasta for lunch, I settled down on the sofa with my laptop, knowing I had at least a few hundred emails waiting for me. I learned that someone had gone through all my settings, and that everything was now encrypted so nobody could trace anything I did online to my whereabouts. Considering that was how my location was discovered before, that was nice, and I wondered why nobody had thought of it sooner. I couldn't even say anything in my own messages about where I was—nothing more specific than the Colorado mountains—or the message would turn to technical gobbledygook, and the receiver wouldn't be able to read it. Apparently, the leaders of Havenwood Falls thought of everything to protect their little town and their big secret.

I spent the afternoon responding to emails and checking out and approving a prototype of a design I'd submitted to a client a couple of weeks ago. I loved seeing my lingerie designs come to life on the kind of models they were created for. Sure, I could sew my own, but I wanted to be sure my lingerie looked good on a variety of big girls, not just those with my body type.

Savage never went far—the farthest being outside for wood. He spent most of his time working out, though. He showed me the extra bedroom he'd converted into a home gym, the reason he didn't have a guest room. After dinner, I did my own workout, but when he came in to join me, it turned into something much more fun that ended in the bedroom.

After, he pulled out an acoustic guitar and played for me by the fire as I sat naked in his bed, sipping wine and watching the snow fall outside.

"I'm not used to an audience," he said almost as an apology, when I clapped after he'd ended a particularly moving rendition of "The Sound of Silence."

"Will you ever cease to surprise me?" I wondered out loud.

"I told you—I have a lot of talents. But stick around long enough, and maybe one day I will."

I stared out the window, not acknowledging that statement. I didn't look over at him until I felt it was safe, and I found him watching the floor, seemingly in deep thought as his fingers strummed of their own accord. Thankfully, they found a familiar tune, and we were both whisked away on the sounds again.

Our days and evenings played out quite similarly for the following week. Niall stopped in regularly to check on me and keep me updated. They'd located the one behind the dark fae attack and were "handling it." I knew what that meant in outlaw-speak, so I asked for no further details. I was just glad that Savage stayed with me and wasn't a part of it.

Of course, I knew he'd killed plenty before. I wasn't an idiot. But I didn't want to be the reason. I'd seen a different side of him that I didn't think too many people knew, and that's *all* I wanted to know. I wouldn't remember him when I left, but for now, I only wanted to think of him as the good guy who kept me safe, fed me, and taught me how to be strong and confident in my most vulnerable state—naked.

CHAPTER 7

I'd been in Havenwood Falls for over a week when Savage went out for much-needed groceries and to run other errands, so I did my laundry while he was away. As I was putting my clean clothes back in my suitcase, I came across the last project I'd been working on when I'd received the call that Pops had been killed. I'd spent my New Year's Day hand-stitching it. I'd forgotten all about it until now, but whoever had packed my bags while I'd been at the funeral must have deemed it worthy of saving. Pulling the slinky black material out, I decided to try it on for the first time.

Studying myself in the mirror, I noticed how the angle of one of the few seams needed to be adjusted and envisioned the effect of moving the cinched ribbon up a couple of inches, to fall right below the breasts, emphasizing them. Perhaps both designs would work. Some bigger women tended to prefer showing off our boobs over drawing attention to our waists, while others tried everything they could to downplay their overly large chests, and then some had little to worry about in that area. That's what so many designers got wrong—big, beautiful women did not fall into one specific shape. We ran the gamut, just like smaller women did. Only recently had the industry started accepting this fact, but there was a long road to travel before it actually embraced our differences.

Lost in my own head and visions, as I tended to get when creating, I never heard the door or the footsteps. I didn't realize I was no longer alone until the voice came into the bedroom and had practically reached the bathroom.

"Tychon Savage, where the hell are you?"

A stunning woman, curvy but much more petite than me, wearing a blue tight-fitting dress that barely covered her bits and four-inch heels, stopped short in front of me as I stood in the bathroom doorway. The fact that the situation was similar to the first night Savage and I hooked up wasn't lost on me. And there was something about this woman that had me imagining doing with her what Savage had done with me that night.

I blinked away the startling thoughts.

"That is fucking gorgeous," she said, staring at me.

"Who the hell are you?" I asked at the same time.

"Melaina Savage," she said as she strutted into the bathroom, checking me out. And for some reason, I let her. Even though— another woman? With his last name? What the hell? "And you must be what's got my brother all jacked up. You wouldn't happen to be a dancer, would you? Because damn, you, wearing that—oh, holy shit. That tattoo! Yeah." She nodded her head as she continued to assess me. "You'd be a knockout on stage."

"*Me?*" Was this woman insane?

She nodded again. "Oh, yeah. Your tits are fabulous. And those curves . . . I have a niche clientele who'd pay out the snout for you."

Her odd choice of words brought me back into focus. "I'm sorry." My hand went to my temple. "Would you mind if I got dressed, and then maybe we could start over?"

"Oh, darlin', don't mind me. I own Silk, the nightclub. And gentlemen's club, and ladies' club, and home of special rooms for the supes, and even more special rooms for the VIPs, if you catch my drift. Trust me—I've seen it all. So go on and get dressed. I just came to grab something out of Tychon's closet. But I really would love to know the name of the designer of the piece you're wearing," she called over her shoulder as she disappeared into his closet.

I was too hung up on her use of Savage's first name to answer her. It'd been the first time I'd heard it. It was a strong name, and quite unusual. Not at all what I expected. Yet another surprise.

Although . . . I couldn't imagine him being a Bob or a Kevin. I internally snickered at the thought.

I'd just gone back into the bedroom to retrieve my clothes when Melaina popped back out. Somehow in the last twelve days, I'd lost much of my modesty. Not only did I not mind that she stood there, all of my bits on full display, but I was kind of turned on by it. What the hell was happening to me? What kind of monster had Savage unleashed in me?

I pulled my clothes on over the lingerie, afraid if I took it off, she'd notice how much she was affecting me.

"Well, at least now I understand why I haven't seen my brother in nearly two weeks," she said as she sauntered for the bedroom door, motioning for me to follow. Her ass swayed beautifully in her skimpy dress, and a part of me hoped the material would ride up just a little more to bare the curve of her cheek.

I shook my head, hard. *Shit.* I'd become a sex-crazed idiot. That's what he'd done to me!

"I can't blame him, though." She went to the kitchen and found our unfinished bottle of wine in the fridge and two glasses. "If I had you in my bed, I wouldn't want to leave, either."

Fortunately, I hadn't taken a sip yet, because I would have blown it out of my nose like the mature lady I was. "Um . . . excuse me?"

She paused as she was about to pour the second glass and looked up at me. "Beauty is beauty—in many shapes and forms, and I, for one, have a true appreciation of it all, regardless of form. And darlin', you're a damn goddess. He'd better be treating you like one."

Heat flushed my face as she passed me a glass. I lifted it to my lips, trying not to down it all in one swallow.

"What do you mean, he's all jacked up?" I asked.

She took her own drink as she studied me with hazel eyes much like his. If she was his sister, which meant she was a hellhound, I wondered why she didn't feel the need to keep her eyes covered. Then I noticed the telltale sign of contacts. Were contacts enough, or were hers a special kind?

"What's your name?" she asked.

"Reyna."

"Well, Reyna, it's not unlike my brother to disappear for a while. We don't exactly keep daily tabs on each other. But he does usually drop into the club on a regular basis, if for no other reason than to check on his boys who work there. Liam's been doing that, though. And he was the one who told me Tychon's been a little . . . not himself. Delegating all his club and business duties. He's even missed church twice this week. And that definitely is not like him. But now I see why."

"Well . . . he's protecting me."

She smiled, her eyes sparkling with a knowing gleam. "He's been doing a lot more than that. I can smell it."

Oh, gods. My face heated again. Hellhounds and their damn sense of smell.

She shook her head. "You really are something else. What's your heritage? Your skin is beautiful."

"I'm from Brazil."

She nodded. "That explains the exotic look. The skin, the dark, almond eyes. I can't blame him one bit. You have that look of being a queen on the streets and a wench in the sheets."

Now I did spit out my wine. "*What?*"

"No judgments here, darlin'. The naughtier the better is my personal belief." She gave me another smile, this one coy as she winked. Then she leaned over the edge of the island, closer to me, her face growing serious. "Just . . . be careful with him, okay? Tychon's been through a lot lately. I don't know if he's okay. And if someone—anyone—fucks him over, they will have to deal with this bitch." Her eyes glowed an orangish red. "And I'm literally a bitch."

Her threat was clear, but I refused to show any fear. Rather, I seized the opportunity to interrogate the one person who might know what he never wanted to talk about. After all, the only way to know how to handle the situation when I left was to know more about it. I sat up straighter and squared my shoulders.

"You mean Addie?" I asked, pinning her with my stare. "He's been through a lot with her?"

She nodded. "Addie. Rachelle . . . that Zandra bitch. It's been a messed up few months around here, and I don't know if he's dealt with it all in a healthy way."

All these women . . . and in a few months?

"How long since he was with her?"

Confusion flickered through her eyes. "He and Lyra? They haven't been together in over a quarter century. They have other issues."

"Lyra?" I had meant Addie, as she seemed to be a recent thing, but now I was curious about yet another name. "Was that his old lady?"

She laughed. "Lyra Beaumont could never be an old lady. That was their problem. But now, I don't think he'll ever have an old lady. Not after he saw what Liam went through with his." She paused, her eyes glazing over. "That loss was unbearable for all of us. And, of course, the mess with Lyra . . ." She focused on me again. "We hellhounds shouldn't breed. Tychon and I are both staunch believers in that."

"What do you mean?"

Her finger traced the edge of her wine glass. "Most females don't survive giving birth, and to be honest, I think that scares the life out of Tychon. Lyra barely made it and only because of magic and taking some seriously drastic measures. Tychon just can't put anyone through that again, and won't put himself through the loss."

"Again?" I asked.

"Addie? Rachelle?"

I shrugged.

"He hasn't told you about them?"

I bit my lip, shaking my head. "He hasn't told me anything. Only that he doesn't currently have a woman. I kind of figured there was something with Addie, although with the way she acts with him, I'm not sure it's healthy."

"No, not at all. They don't exactly have a close relationship. I mean, she just found out he was her father about a year ago. Up until then, they knew *of* each other, names and such, but not even really acquaintances."

I managed to swallow my wine this time before I gave her another shower. "Her *father*? Addie's his *daughter*?"

She nodded. "Rachelle, too. Addie didn't know about Rachelle, either, and she'd run away years ago. None of them were ever close." She sighed. "Like I said, it's been a big complicated mess. And with Rachelle's death last month . . . I'm just not sure how he's dealing with it all."

Holy. Shit. Savage had lost his daughter not too long before I'd lost my Pops. And he hadn't said anything. Hadn't even mentioned he had daughters, even after I'd met one of them. An array of emotions swept through me, most of them sadness for the man they called Savage.

Melaina watched as I blinked away tears of sorrow. I turned my head to swipe at my eyes and draw in a steadying breath. When I turned back, Melaina was pouring herself more wine.

"Look. He probably hasn't told you any of this because he didn't want you to know," she said. "And he might kill me, but I think you should. You need to know what you're getting into. And he needs someone who can be there for him as he puts his pieces back together, not break him all over again. Because I'm afraid of what he'll become otherwise. I never thought I'd say this, but Tychon Savage needs salvation. He needs to know love again."

I stared at the counter, letting this sink in, then I grabbed for the bottle and drank straight from it. I finally looked up at her, into her hazel eyes with that orange glow still in the depths of them.

"I can't be his salvation. My own situation is way too messed up. But I don't think you have to worry about me breaking him. We're not like that."

"Are you sure about that?"

"Positive."

She studied me for a long moment, then shrugged. "Too bad. I think I could really like you. But I'm well versed in the need for a little fun in the sack as a distraction. If you're ever interested in something different . . ."

Her voice trailed off right before the door opened, and Savage and Niall strode in, each carrying several sacks of groceries.

"Get your own," Savage growled at his sister, and Melaina laughed before taking in Niall.

As her eyes roved over him, the sexual energy she'd already been exuding intensified exponentially, doing strange and not entirely unwelcome things to my body.

"Mmm . . . maybe I will." She winked at Niall before sauntering through the door they'd left open, swinging those shapely hips of hers. "Thanks for the key, brother," she called out before closing the door behind her.

Niall watched through the side window. "Bloody hell. Wouldn't mind a taste of that arse."

"That's my sister," Savage rumbled.

Niall turned and glanced at me, then at Savage with an arched brow. "And payback's a bitch, brutha."

I TRIED NOT to let Melaina's words affect me, but I couldn't completely erase them from my mind, either. Savage hadn't shared that personal information with me for a reason—he knew there was no need for me to know. We'd both agreed that we had no intentions of anything beyond the short term happening between us, and that wasn't the kind of shit you shared with a fling. And laying such heavy stuff on someone you might never see again wasn't fair to either of you or the fun and distraction you were trying to create. So acting any differently, treating him any differently wouldn't have been right to him or what we had.

But when the stray thoughts made their way in, my heart hurt. I'd seen enough past the savage beast to the man inside to understand what Melaina meant. A part of me wished I could be the woman he needed, but I knew myself too well. Our worlds were too different, and I could never fit in his.

"Nice blog post today," he said a couple of nights later as we hung out on the sofa, me working on my laptop and him tossing his tablet onto the coffee table. His hair was pulled back in a man bun —a style I normally despised, but he made it work extremely well— and he wore nothing but sweat pants as he lounged on the other part of the L-shaped sectional, looking more like a model than a biker.

"You read my blog?" I asked with surprise.

"Every post you've ever made. It's changed a lot over the years. Evolved."

I stared at him with a slack jaw. He looked over at me and smiled. "I shocked you again, didn't I?"

"Um . . . yeah. Why the hell did you do that? I mean, unless you have some secret cross-dressing life or something?"

He shrugged. "I like lingerie."

"Oh. So it was for the pictures." That at least made sense.

"And I like your words."

I rolled my eyes, but smiled on the inside. "I'd love to do a write-up about Callie's shop, but that's probably not allowed."

"That's something the Court would decide."

Right. The Court of the Sun and the Moon—the decision makers Addie had told me about when she'd been dragging tiny needles over my skin. The ones who kept the registry and made sure everyone stayed in line.

"They have ways to draw the tourists in without giving us away. But you'd have to get on their good side first."

I didn't foresee that happening. I imagined that took time, to build their trust, and I didn't plan on spending much time here. Although, I really hadn't had a chance to explore yet.

"You should go back into town," Savage said, as though he'd read my mind. "Get to know it better."

"I've been busy with work. Besides, I didn't think it was allowed."

"Mmm . . . well . . ." His mouth pulled to the side. "Would you be mad if I just really didn't want to share you?" He winked at me before I could respond, softening the blow. "I'll take you tomorrow," he added quickly.

"So you can stalk me around the shops and breathe down my neck again, scaring everyone away?"

The corner of his lips curled upward in a smirk. "I thought you liked me breathing down your neck . . . and other places."

A chill ran up my spine. "You know what I mean."

He sat up, turning to set his feet on the ground. "No worries. I don't want the wrath of Addie again."

"The wrath of Addie?"

"You didn't see that fit she threw that night? Chewed me a new asshole about how Torq and me were scaring off everyone's customers and then went on about how you needed 'space and independence.'" He dropped those last three words with quotes, although he didn't do the air quote thing. I could hear them. "So I'll take you into town tomorrow, and you can have your space and independence."

"It's safe?" I asked.

"As long as you stay within the wards, yeah."

I leaned back. "So you let Addie chew you a new asshole, huh?"

And for some reason—maybe he was just in a talkative mood that night—he spilled everything Melaina had told me and more. He gave more details about Addie and Rachelle that sounded more like a soap opera than real life. He told me about his agreement with Lyra to never tell Addie until the appropriate time came, and how he could watch over her from a distance, but couldn't be a part of her life as she grew up. He talked little of Rachelle, only explaining how a friend of the family had raised her in another town, that he could have been a part of her life, but she wanted little to do with him and then ran away. Amends had never been made between them before they lost her again. He told me about Liam and his wife, and how she'd died after their third son was born. How badly it had wrecked Liam.

"Wow," I breathed. "I've never loved anyone like that." I didn't know if I ever could, either. Not with my . . . situation. I peered over at him. "Have you?"

He pondered his feet propped up on the coffee table. "Like Liam and Savannah? No. I might have come close twice. Once with Lyra and once in the 1700s."

"1700s?" I murmured. I hadn't realized how old he was. Supes were so weird in that way. Pops and Niall were way older than they looked, so I was kind of used to it, but still, I now felt like an infant.

Savage's lids lifted, his eyes raising to me. "You remind me of them, in certain ways."

"I do? How?" *Gods, please don't say anything that's going to make me cave.*

"You're an old soul, like both of them. Intelligent. Witty. Sassy. Wise beyond your years. Born to be leaders." He stood and walked over to the window, placing his hands on his hips. His voice came out low, still rumbly but the edge softened. "Another fascinating female too good for me. I always want what I can't have."

Oh, fookin' hell.

As usual, we couldn't keep our hands off each other when we crawled into bed. The mind-blowing sex had remained just that—mind-blowing. Over the past two weeks, we'd done things I'd never done before. We experimented. We had fun. My inner beast pushed at the surface, making me wild.

But tonight . . . tonight was different. Not in a bad way. Not. At. All. In fact, it might have been the most amazing time yet. When I yelled out "Tychon" instead of "Savage" on my climax, he froze for a moment as our eyes locked, and when he continued, something was different. I couldn't put my finger on it, but something was changing. Something between us.

CHAPTER 8

Savage was gone when I awoke the next morning, having left a note by the coffee maker saying that he had to go on a CDI run. I had to wonder if that was the full truth or if he'd euphemized a club job because he knew my feelings about it. Niall texted me, saying he was also going on the run, but as long as I stayed within the town's wards I'd be safe—though he preferred if I just stayed home. By mid-afternoon, though, I hadn't heard from either of them, and I was tired of working on Savage's couch . . . or at the kitchen island . . . or on the chaise longue by the fireplace in the bedroom. My creativity for drawing had dried up, none of the designs in my head translating well to the sketchbook. I was also bored with the home gym equipment and longed for fresh air.

I replaced my black dress pants and silk blouse with fleece-lined leggings, a hoodie, thick socks and hiking boots, and the ugly but warm puffy ski jacket. A quick search in Savage's coat closet led me to an extra beanie hat—a Harley-Davidson one, of course, but it would have to do. I was going hiking.

I didn't plan to go too far. I wasn't stupid. It was the middle of winter, the mountains were treacherous, and the woods vast. I understood it could be easy to get lost. But that was the benefit of having an inner animal with extraordinary senses and a sharpened instinct. Besides, I was only going to go down to the creek by the cemetery that I could see from the house and come right back up. I figured that would be a decent enough workout.

As I picked my way down the slope, slipping and sliding in some places, that inner beast begged for release. Once I made it to the creek, my kelpie, a water creature, reared its head with intensified interest. Inhaling deeply, I caught an intriguing scent that made my nostrils flare and my heart pick up speed. It was crisp and sweet at the same time, calling to me like a frozen drink on the beach. The intriguing smell came from nearly straight north from where I stood, if I had my directions right, which I was pretty sure I did—the scent of frozen water with a hint of something else. Something that made my senses tingle with exalted anticipation, that pulled me toward it like a magnet.

I couldn't say how long I hiked—an hour, maybe less, maybe much more—until my feet landed on a path that took me straight to where my soul pulled. As I rounded a copse of evergreens and stepped into the clearing, I gasped at the sight before me. She looked like a bride rising hundreds of feet up the cliff, her dress a frozen mass cascading down into a pool of ice. There was only a slight trickle along the massive icicles that created a small hole in the frozen pond at the bottom of the falls. This must have been the great falls that gave the town its name.

The sight was probably beautiful in warmer weather, but it was breathtaking almost completely frozen over—what one might call a once-in-a-lifetime view, although, I supposed, not for the people who called this town home. I wondered how many actually came out to appreciate its beauty. I was glad nobody did now.

Because it wasn't the beauty that had drawn me here. How could it have been, since I hadn't seen it yet? It was something in that water. Something that called to me. A source of magic that had my kelpie bucking inside me, demanding to be freed. Something I didn't want to share with a single soul.

I slowly stepped toward the edge of the pond, scanning the area to double-check for other life. Boulders bordered the water and beyond them were woods of evergreens and thin white aspen trunks. The mountain climbed up sharply from here. The sky above was already turning from blue to a light shade of purple, the sun already behind the mountains to the west. I sniffed, but that intoxicating scent was all I could pick up—no trace of anyone nearby.

Climbing up to sit on one of the boulders, I swung my legs around and gingerly tested the ice with one foot, pressing on it to see if it was as solid as it looked. Deciding it could hold my weight, I carefully walked toward the hole, but the closer I came, the less I worried. Why was I even concerned? I was a creature of the water. If I fell in, I wouldn't drown. Once I was close, I dropped to my knees and pulled off my mittens. Reaching forward, I scooped my hand into the hole.

Magic zinged up my arm and throughout my body.

The ice around me cracked and fell away.

I plunged into the freezing water, my arms and legs flailing as I gasped for air before submersing completely.

But then, I was no longer me.

Not human me.

Kelpie me.

Unicorn me.

Something had caused me to lose all control. I didn't even have a chance to calm her and try to keep her contained. One moment I was human, and the next I was not.

With powerful muscles, I sprang out of the water and onto the ice, galloping across it to the boulders. Once on land, I shook myself out, spraying the nearby tree trunks with water that quickly became ice crystals.

Free! I was fucking *free*!

I wanted to shout it—whinny it—whatever. I'd never felt such elation in my life. I'd kept her trapped inside for entirely too long, and this week, when my animalism had been at its most basic, she'd been kicking and thrashing to be released. It had been years, and now, finally, she was out. I'd thought it'd been my time with Savage that was calling so loudly to her, but maybe it had been this place all along—these falls, this water.

I bucked and reared and pranced in and around the trees. I desperately wanted to run and run and *run*. Maybe never come back.

But the water still drew me to it. I moseyed back over to the pond and stood on a boulder, gazing down at my reflection—an all-black hide with a silver mane and tail and a silvery, glimmering horn spiraling out of my head. I was magnificent. Nothing this beautiful should have to be imprisoned.

Sadly, that was my lot in life, though. And I knew I needed to rein her back in, pull her into me, and return to my human form. I didn't know what to do about my clothes that appeared to be floating in the freezing water on the far side of the pond, but if I were ever seen like this—

As though on cue, a gasp sounded from behind me.

"Are you real?" the male voice whispered, and I turned around to find a man peeking out from behind a tree, his eyes large as plates as he stared at me with fascination.

Shit. Fuck. Damn. And every other word in the book.

I should have run. Or I should have charged after him, hoping to scare him off and make him wonder if he'd really seen what he thought he had.

But I didn't.

I stood frozen, staring at him as he stared at me. Then that animal intuition picked up on something about him. Something not right. In fact, something very wrong. My kelpie instinct kicked in, and there was nothing I could do to stop myself. As much as I tried to turn the other way, my legs carried me forward to him, and as I approached, he stepped out from behind the tree, just as drawn to me as I was to him. His hand reached out. His fingers brushed over the fringes of my mane, and then his palm settled on my side. And that was all it took.

Nothing but instinct—my prime purpose as a kelpie—controlled me, turning me toward the pond, pulling the guy with me.

"Hey! What the hell?" He yelled and thrashed, but once he'd touched me, he'd signed his own death warrant. The water in my fur became like super-glue, of the supernatural kind. Nothing he nor I did could free him. I would haul him into the water, take him down into its depths, and not release him until he drowned. It was the terrible and terrifying side of my nature.

My hooves lugged us over the boulders, and I tried to force myself to stop, but I couldn't. My kelpie had taken over. She was in complete control. We dragged him over the ice as he continued to fight me and I tried to fight myself.

No! I silently screamed. *We won't kill him! We don't kill!*

I threw myself at my kelpie, and her body bucked, but she continued on. I cried out, a whinny in the night, tossing my head side to side. But she continued on. As hard as I tried to pull her back into me and become human again, she fought me even harder. This was what my kind was meant to do, and there was no way to stop her. Even as our hooves dragged across the ice, she continued on.

The man shouted for help, twisting and turning, and begging for release. Then I felt a sharp pain in my flank. His free arm swung outward, and in my peripheral vision, I saw a dagger in his hand. The dumb ass had stabbed me! He shouldn't have been able to, though. That was no ordinary blade. It had to have been infused with magic to pierce my hide.

I reared back, tossing him in the air, but never losing my hold on him. His free hand arced down again for another slice, across my hindquarter this time, and I jumped and bucked.

Even as we fought, though, she continued on.

When agony screamed from my withers and up my neck from another carving through my flesh, this one much deeper, I threw my head back with a cry. And I no longer cared if we drowned him, because if he plunged the blade into my throat next time, we would both die. So I twisted my neck backward, trying to catch the right angle to spear him with my horn.

But my front hooves had hit the edge of the ice, and it cracked behind us. The piece we were on teetered forward, rocking down into the water. No matter what, he was going to die. I'd known it from the moment I'd sensed that darkness in him, whether I wanted him to or not. But now I did.

As I was about to plunge us downward, a huge fireball streaked toward us, slamming into my accidental rider. His agonizing scream indicated much more than the pain I'd felt, and his body went limp. I turned just in time to see the fiery blaze, nearly as big as me, fly at us again. I whinnied loudly, throwing myself sideways, but the fire slammed into the man, and this time carried him off.

And I knew what that meant.

My kelpie couldn't release him until—unless—he was dead.

I galloped across the pond to the bank where the fireball had stopped. And I realized it wasn't a fireball at all, but a hound almost the size of my kelpie form, flames shining out of its eyes, nose, and mouth. Its skin contained an orange glow that defined its thick muscles, as though the fire burnt within rather than on the surface. It stared at me with those orangish-red eyes, smoke rising from its body and billowing out of its mouth between six-inch fangs as it panted.

My attacker lay on the ground in a pool of blood flowing from his ravaged throat, shredded skin and tendons all that remained of it, the hound hovering over him.

We regarded each other in a standoff. I wondered if that was Savage in there—or somebody else. I'd never seen a hellhound before, but this looked like it could definitely be one, and the rotten-egg smell of sulfur and brimstone wafted on the air. I'd nearly taken a life. Was this beast here to escort my soul to Hell?

If I shifted now, I'd surely die. I looked from side to side, wondering if I could make a break for it—and if that would be any better. Running would improve my chance of someone else seeing me, and either they'd take me or I'd kill them. Staying, though, would improve my chance of dying.

The hellhound moved.

Dropping my head, I pawed at the ground and snorted, my breath big plumes not unlike the smoke from the hound.

Then its shape twisted and morphed . . . and a moment later, Savage knelt close to the ground.

He rose to his large, gloriously naked body's full height and took a step forward. I exhaled again. He lifted his hands, slowly, palms out. To show he meant no harm, to calm me. His gaze roved over me.

"Reyna?" he asked, his raspy tone genuinely curious—a mix of uncertainty that it was actually me with wonder at what he was seeing. He must not have known what I really was, after all. He took another step closer, and I stepped back. "Mother fucker. You're hurt."

I was, but I was healing. The longer I stayed in this form, the less I'd suffer when I took my human shape.

A neigh from the woods had my head jerking in that direction. A black horse trotted into the clearing, and I recognized the kelpie. Niall.

"Reyna, my queen," he said into my mind. *"You're okay."*

I tilted my head toward the hellhound.

"It's okay. It's over. Savage saved you."

"No! He killed for me. Someone else died because of me!"

"He would have died because of you anyway."

"Niall, get her to fucking shift," Savage ordered. "You need to take her home before the rest find us."

"You heard him, Rey. You can't be seen."

My kelpie balked, not wanting to lose herself again, not knowing the next time she could be released. She reared and bucked as I struggled to pull her back in, but footsteps in the distance, the snapping of twigs under heavy boots, and the odor of more brimstone sent us into a panic—fear of being seen but also of being tempted to kill—and she finally submitted. My muscles and bones screamed in pain as they shrunk and reformed themselves. My insides felt like they were shredded as my organs reshaped and rearranged. It shouldn't be this painful, the result of not shifting often enough. I was left shivering and panting in a tight ball on the ground.

Something heavy draped over me. I dared to lift my head, my still-healing skin searing with the movement, to find Savage standing over me, covering me with clothes. His clothes. I had no idea where they came from, but I noticed he stood between Niall and me, blocking me from Niall's view. If I wasn't such a physical and emotional mess, I would have laughed at his chivalry.

"Let Niall take you home," he said quietly as he leaned down to pull the shirt on the rest of the way and help me stand. He gripped my face with both hands, his eyes searching mine as though hunting for some kind of answer, but I didn't know the question. There was something in his I couldn't quite decipher. Something I'd never seen before. "Hurry. Get the fuck out of here. Others are coming fast."

With that, he lifted me up by the waist and placed me on Niall's back, slapping the kelpie's hindquarters. Good thing hellhounds were immune to the kelpie's kill instinct, or we would have had more problems. Instead, Niall shot his hind leg out and kicked Savage as we took off, not appreciating the smack on the ass.

Gods. I didn't know who would be more humiliated when this was over—me for riding Niall or Niall for having been ridden.

"*I would do anything for you,*" Niall said as he trotted through the woods. At least if he were seen, people would only see a woman on a horse—a half-naked woman in the dead of winter, but that was much less worrisome than their sighting of a unicorn. "*There's only one other ass I'd allow on my back, but for you, my queen, anything.*"

I tried to tell him to stop calling me that, but the skin of my neck pulled too much when I opened my mouth.

"*I can still hear your thoughts,*" he informed me.

Oh. "*Well, then, stop calling me queen.*"

"*Did you see yourself, love? You're majestic. Everyone should call you that.*"

"*If you do, I'll shank you.*"

He snorted.

A shiver racked through my body, and Niall picked up the pace. His body was warm, but not like Savage's. I pushed aside thoughts of him. Thoughts I didn't want Niall eavesdropping on.

Once we were back at Savage's cabin, I hurried inside even before Niall shifted. A hot shower was all I could think about, at least until Niall could no longer hear my thoughts. I felt it in my consciousness when his mind disconnected from mine, and I sighed with relief as I turned the water on, letting my thoughts run. As the water heated, I gave myself a quick once-over in the mirror. The wound on my butt was now only a red welt. The one on my side, just above my hip, a small scar. The gash on my neck had been the worst, and it was already mostly healed, the skin still tight and somewhat sore, but the wound closed and scabbed over. Only a centimeter or two over or deeper, and he would have hit my jugular, killing me. My muscles, joints, and bones hurt more from the transformation than any of my injuries. I gingerly stepped under the hot water, but it felt too good to notice the burn on my wounds.

No matter how long I stood under its warmth, though, I couldn't stop shaking. No longer from the cold, but from the thoughts running amok in my mind and the emotional upheaval they brought.

I didn't know if I was more sickened by what I'd almost done or that Savage had finished the job for me. I feared what would happen next. What the repercussions would be for us. Addie had made it clear that humans couldn't know about the supes, and I'd let one see me. And he'd died because of it. Now Savage would have to suffer whatever punishment their Court gave. I could handle banishment. It wasn't like I'd planned to stay anyway. But this was his home, his family, his life. If he didn't hate me for it, I'd hate myself enough for the both of us.

All because I'd decided to go for a fucking hike.

"Reyna?" Savage's gravelly voice jolted me out my mind.

Without waiting for me to respond, he stepped into the shower with me. His eyes traveled from my head to my toes, lingering on what was left of my wounds. Relief filled his features as his arms snaked around my back, and he pulled me up against his body, enveloping me with all that was Savage. He felt strong, protective, and comforting, and I leaned into him, a sob escaping. He held me tighter as I cried into his chest.

He stepped back when the sobs finally stopped and lifted my chin to look up at him. "Better?"

"Why did you do it?" I asked, more tears forming in my eyes. "Why did you kill him?"

"Because you were about to."

"I didn't want to!"

"I know."

My brows squeezed together, my head shaking. "I don't

understand. What? Are you so okay with killing that you just had to do it instead? Kill an innocent?"

Now his brows dropped low. "First of all, he wasn't an innocent. He was wanted by the Court for rape and murder. And no, I'm not that okay with killing, regardless of what others say and think. But I do what I have to do."

"But you didn't have to! If he had it coming anyway, you should have just let me do it."

His warm breath fanned over me with a heavy sigh. "Honestly, I hadn't intended to kill him. The Court wanted him dead. That's why they keep us around—to serve as their bounty hunters and executioners. And I'm usually the one to do the takedown. Something kept going through my mind as we hunted for him, though." His eyes bounced between mine. "You, Reyna—thinking you'd be waiting for me at home. And I decided I wasn't going to be the one this time. I couldn't see myself being able to look into your eyes afterward."

"Then *why*? Why did you? And so . . . so *gruesomely*. So—"

"Savagely?" he offered, and I gulped, nodding. "Because any of my other ways would have killed you, too. And when I saw that beautiful creature, I just knew it was you, injured and bleeding but about to serve him justice. And I just couldn't let you do that."

I jutted my chin out. "Well, you should have."

"Don't you get it?" he growled, his hands grasping the sides of my face, holding me still as his gaze pierced into mine. "That's *why* I had to. You're not a killer, Reyna. I couldn't let that one moment in time forever change who you are. I couldn't let it darken your pristine soul."

I blinked away the forming tears and water pouring down my face, my anger sluicing down to the drain with it.

"And what about yours?" I murmured. "I'm supposed to accept that I let yours grow even darker with yet another kill?"

A smirk curled his lips as he blew out a breath. "Sweetheart, I'm a creature of Hell. My soul can't get any blacker than it was the day I was born." He dropped one palm from my face to land on my chest. "But yours . . . it's beautiful and pure."

I shook my head. "You don't know that."

"Hellhound here. I see souls." He leaned in, his rock-hard cock pressing into my belly as his mouth dropped near my ear. "And you are fucking glorious, inside and out."

His lips and hot breath on my ear sent a shiver down my spine. The hand on my chest slid to my breast, cupping it, my nipple immediately pebbling against his palm. The other went behind my head, twisting into my hair and pulling, tilting my face up to him.

"I need to fuck you now, Reyna," he said, leaving no room for argument.

CHAPTER 9

*N*ot that I wanted to argue. I was completely defenseless as his mouth crashed on mine, his tongue thrusting between my lips, parting them. I matched his need, his intensity. After everything that happened, I understood the desperation for human contact, for some kind of release of the buildup and tension of the day. My hands latched on to his thick shoulders, pulling him closer for more skin-to-skin contact. His hand between us squeezed my breast almost too hard . . . almost. I tasted him as he tasted me. Bit his lip as he bit mine. When he began to pull away for a breath, I pressed harder into him, my tongue sweeping over his full lips, my mouth sucking the water that dripped over them.

His cock was like a steel rod between us, and I slipped my hand over it, curling my fingers around the head, then sliding down the thick shaft. A low growl rumbled deep in his throat. It turned me the hell on. I needed to hear it again. Still stroking him, I slowly lowered myself before him, my mouth skimming over his wet beard, his neck, his ridiculously sculpted chest and abs, until I was on my knees before him. My other hand slid over his sack, cupping his balls, as I took his head in my mouth.

"Fuck, Reyna," he growled, making my core clench.

I took him in farther, my tongue swirling and stroking as my

83

hands also worked him until he gripped my head, and he was thrusting into my mouth. I matched his rhythm, tasting him as he was about to come, sucking hard so he would, but then he jerked away. He suddenly stood on the other side of the large shower, out of my reach.

"As much as I like fucking your mouth, I need to fuck *you*."

Good gods, that was hot.

With a small nod and knowing what he liked, I turned around on my knees, and bracing my forearms on the built-in bench, I rose onto my feet, lifting my ass high in the air for him. He didn't hesitate. He palmed it with both hands, squeezing and kneading my flesh as he moved closer behind me. One thumb slid between my crack and over my hole, pausing to press against it, making my hips buck up toward him. He always teased me there, but never entered. I never asked him to—even being touched there was new to me—but each time, my curiosity grew as I fantasized about what it would feel like to have him inside what I'd always thought to be my Do Not Enter Zone.

He moved on before I could decide whether to say anything this time, his fingers coasting through my wet folds, circling around my entry before continuing on to tease and taunt the already swollen bundle of nerves. I whimpered and moaned, my legs trembling and jerking. Then two fingers entered, and my pelvis jerked. They curled and hit the G-spot perfectly, making me cry out and thrust backward.

"Fuck me, Savage," I begged. "Please . . . fuck me. Everywhere."

"Everywhere?" he rumbled as his hand moved faster, stroking in and out, one finger still working my clit furiously.

"Gods, yes! Everywhere!"

His other hand skated over my ass, moving to tease my puckered hole. "Here?"

My core clenched around his fingers inside me just at the thought of it. I'd done so much with him. Things I never imagined doing before. Why not this, too? Why not go all out? It was so dirty. So naughty. So taboo, in my head. And at this moment, so necessary.

"Please!" I shouted.

He growled, low and sexy as hell, the sound of a virile beast, making my breasts swell tightly against my skin. Then he gave a slight push, and I cried out as I was stretched and full in all the places. The sensations—the pressure on my clit, his fingers stroking my pussy, the fullness and tightness in my ass, even my nipples sliding over my forearm—were overwhelming. I lost it. My body moved of its own accord, because my mind was gone. Completely fucking gone. My hands grasped my breasts, pinching and rolling my nipples, as my legs rocked and bounced, increasing the friction inside me. It was all so sensuous . . . so erotic . . . so . . . so . . . oh, *gods*, so explosive. He made my body shatter around him and beg for more at the same time, until all I could do was scream his name over and over as I soared away on the final wave of ecstasy.

My trembling legs gave way, but Savage caught me before I hit the ground. His arms scooped under my knees and around my shoulders, and he carried me out of the shower, our wet bodies dripping a trail over the floor as he crossed the bathroom and went to the bed. He gently lowered me in the center and crawled over me. His long wet locks fell forward as he closed his mouth over mine. But not for nearly long enough. I wanted to taste him more, devour him even, but he moved down.

His sodden beard and warm tongue skated over my neck and collarbone. He took precious time on each breast, and my body quaked, whether still with aftershocks or with renewed need, I didn't know. One was flowing into the other, especially as his mouth lowered, his tongue swirling around my belly button before moving on to the crease between my pelvis and leg, then he sucked the inside of one thigh and the other before pushing my legs wide. Then, oh, gods, his mouth closed over my already pulsing sex and sucked, and I lifted myself against his face, about to lose it again.

Before I did, my fingers entangled in his hair and pulled him up. "I need your cock."

He smirked before flattening his tongue and swiping it up my folds, twirling it around my hole, making me gasp. "And I needed to taste you."

He took another long, languid taste before rising on his hands and moving back upward. He held himself over me on his hands and knees, his gaze a weighty caress up my body, full of such promises that could never be spoken aloud. When his eyes came back to mine, we locked onto each other. His became unreadable as he moved his knees between mine. He straightened his legs behind him, lowering his hips, our gazes still holding as his cock pressed into my opening. Then his eyes fell shut as he gradually slid inside me.

So thick.

So long.

So perfect.

So excruciatingly slow.

He'd said he needed to fuck me before, but this . . . this was not fucking. Not like we had every other time, not even last night. This was . . . so different. Something had definitely changed. He drew out his strokes, taking his time filling me up again and then withdrawing just as slowly. My heart raced from the massive orgasm he'd already given me, but my body easily fell into the more leisurely pace, rocking with him, each torturously slow movement in and out increasing the sensation exponentially, causing waves of chills to run over my flesh.

His arms slid under me, gathering me into his chest, my breasts pressed between us, his face nuzzling into my neck and shoulder, his mouth wet against my skin. My arms curled under his and up around his back. Somehow, without releasing or losing any contact, we shifted to sit up, me on top, my legs wrapped around him. We continued moving together, my nipples rubbing deliciously against his chest, his hands stroking up and down my back. One slid up and wrapped around my hair, pulling. My head fell, and my back arched, giving his mouth access to my breasts. He didn't disappoint, his tongue swirling over my nipple, his teeth grazing over it, then his mouth pulling it within. My hips rocked harder, trying to pick up the pace as my need continued building.

He shifted us again, starting the build all over.

My inexperienced self thought we'd done pretty well in trying out all the different positions during our time together, but tonight we explored even more. More intimate than ever. More pleasurable than ever. Still luxuriously slow. Still somehow different.

At some point, I ended up on my back again, in the only position I'd ever personally experienced before Savage. Back to the basics. But it was far from basic with him. With us. As my hips lifted to meet his, he gazed at me with hooded lids. Our eyes locked again, something passed between us, and he began to quicken the pace. His weight on his elbows, his hands cupped my face.

"Reyna," he moaned as he thrust inside me before pulling out. "My Reyna." He drove in hard again and then wrenched out. Our eyes held as our breaths came faster, my hips rolling up with each of his strokes inward, pulling back when he did. Our movements quickly escalated, reaching an urgent pace, our pelvises slamming together. "My unicorn," he groaned as he rammed into me, my core squeezing around him. And then as we climbed to our climax, he growled with each hard thrust, "Mine. Mine. Mine."

And as everything within me came apart again, I got caught up in the wondrous moment, and my mind already far over the edge, I shouted as I came, "Yours. Yours. *Yours.*"

I climaxed first, but he was right after me, closing his eyes and still moaning *mine.* We floated down, and he collapsed on top of me, his body trembling. Rolling off to my side, he wrapped his arms around me and pulled me close, whispering my name as we both drifted off.

MY EYES POPPED open as the realization hit me. I'd been sound asleep one moment and wide awake the next when it came to me—why sex with Savage had felt different tonight. I'd chalked up the "mine" possessive bullshit to the heat of the moment, but even now as I realized the truth, that claim of ownership explained the change. He'd said he needed to fuck me when we were in the shower, but that's not what we did. We hadn't been two people just having a good time, scratching an itch, meeting a need. Not tonight.

We'd languished in it. We'd explored every inch of each other not only in an erotic way but with care and adoration. We drew it out, relishing how the other felt against us, around us, within us. And not

87

just physically. The connection was deeper this time. More real. We were using our bodies to express how we felt . . . emotionally.

We were making love.

Oh, gods. Did Tychon Savage love me? Did I love him?

The thoughts had me squirming, and I tried to sneak out of bed, but Savage's arms wrapped tighter around me, his face nuzzling into the back of my neck. I froze. Was he awake? His breathing remained steady. I relaxed, but I couldn't go back to sleep, my mind reeling.

Did he possibly love me? Was he even capable of it anymore? He'd sounded like he'd given up on the emotion and all that it entailed ever since Addie's mother, Lyra. He'd been with other women since then, of course, but none that captured him beyond the physical. So why me? There was nothing extraordinary about me . . . except that I was a unicorn. And he'd called me *his* unicorn. Had seeing me in my other form changed the way he felt about me? Or was it a ploy, now that he knew what I was and therefore my street value, so that I *would* be his unicorn?

I mentally shook that thought away. It wasn't a fair accusation to harp on, for him or for me, because my self-esteem didn't need that kind of negative self-talk.

And there was a very good chance everything had been one-sided. Maybe only I had felt the difference because the change had only been in me. I didn't know if I loved him—it was too soon and the thought too terrifying to dwell on—but I did know I'd developed some kind of feelings for him, and that just couldn't possibly happen. We couldn't be together. There were too many things against us. For one, I was not old lady material, no matter how good he'd tried to make it sound, and he wasn't going to give up his life as a biker for me. I wouldn't want him to. That was too much a part of who he was—it was one half of the dichotomy of Tychon Savage that I liked so much. The man I was . . . falling for.

And for two, I was not staying here in Havenwood Falls. Tonight was proof that not even this place was safe for me—and definitely not for anyone else. This had never been a long-term solution for me. New Orleans was my home—the sultry South, the bayou, the accents, the music, the Garden District, the French Quarter, the beignets and seafood and red beans and rice and gumbo . . . I could go on and on just about the food. That was my home. Not this remote town in the mountains.

Then why haven't you so much as given it a second thought for over a week now?

I ignored that voice. Staying was not something I should be trying to talk myself into. No. I needed to make plans to go home, and I spent the rest of the night formulating a mental checklist until I finally drifted off again, not to wake until after noon.

"You good?" Savage asked as I sat at the kitchen island with my coffee. "You've been quiet today."

I looked up at him and smiled. "Just tired. Still a little sore."

His lips turned up in a smirk, and he winked at me. Yeah, he was part of the reason for being sore, the part I didn't mind. Regardless of my epiphany in the middle of the night, I didn't regret one moment I'd spent with Savage. He'd done so much for me, more than he would ever know or even understand. He would be a good memory to hold on to—the man who turned this near-virgin queen on the streets into an uninhibited wench in the sheets.

"Take a nap. Or go to bed early. I don't know how long I'll be. We have church, and then Liam and I gotta meet with the Court tonight, give them the story about what happened last night."

"They're going to want to meet with me, too, aren't they?" Part of me kind of hoped they would banish me, because that would make this whole thing a lot easier.

"Not if I can help it. They got what they wanted. I did it. They won't even know you were involved." He came around the island and kissed my temple before going over to grab his leather coat. "Your secret is safe."

I sucked in my bottom lip, biting the flesh to keep it from trembling as emotion swept through me. Blinking, I looked away, toward the windows, but my gaze stopped as I noticed a dresser sitting in the living room near the bedroom door. It hadn't been there before.

"Where did that come from and why is it there?" It was a beautiful piece—a lot like the furniture I'd had in my own apartment, but the style didn't fit in here, especially not where it stood now.

Savage followed my gaze and turned back to give me another wink. "Brought it back from yesterday's CDI run. I thought you might be tired of living out of suitcases."

Oh, damn. The tears rose, and I blinked rapidly to keep them away.

"Hey." He moved back over to me and lifted my chin with his finger. "We'll talk about it later. No assumptions. Just know you're welcome here. Always. For as long as you like."

I nodded, unable to speak. Well, that answered that question—the feelings weren't one-sided, and his weren't because he'd discovered what I was. He'd bought the dresser, thinking of me, before he'd known.

He shoved his arms through his coat sleeves, studying me the whole time. "Reyna, seriously. Don't fucking worry about it. I'll take care of it when I get home." He leaned over and kissed me on the mouth this time. "I promise not to wake you if you're sleeping." His lips turned up. "Unless you want me to, then leave me a note."

He bent down for another kiss, and I leaned up into it, savoring it, committing to memory his taste, his scent, his touch, the way his tongue felt against mine, how his fingers pressed into my hips, tightening his hold.

And as I watched him stride out the door, I recalled sadly that I wouldn't remember him when I left. I wouldn't remember any of this.

CHAPTER 10

*W*hen I was sure he was gone, I let the dam burst and cried into my coffee. Then I renewed my resolve and sent a text to Niall.

Me: What are you doing? I need a ride.

Niall: about to go into church

Me: How long?

Niall: no idea but gotta go to court with them too since I was there

Me: Shit. Does this place have Uber? Or can you get me a taxi?

Niall: where you going

Me: Is it safe to leave town yet?

Niall: fuck no need another week or two

Niall: why you talking about leaving anyway?

Me: I need to get out of here

Niall: outta the house?

Me: for good

My phone went silent for a while, and I wondered if he'd gone into the club's meeting. Or worse, if he was asking Savage what happened to make me want to leave.

Niall: rey, you fuckin ghosting him?

Now I hesitated with a reply. Part of me wanted to, but I'd hate myself for it. Once I had some space and could gather my thoughts to share them properly, I'd let Savage know and give us a clean break. Deep down, he had to know it was coming.

Me: I'll talk to him later, after I'm out. I need space first.

Niall: They have luber here

Me: Uber? Can you get one for me? I can't get the app on my phone

Niall: No, luber not uber

Me: Luber? Ew!

Niall: yeah as bad as you're imagining, they said

Me: Who? You didn't say anything to him, did you?

Niall: course not

Niall: gotta go church starting I'll ask about a truck

Damn. I didn't know how long they'd be meeting, and then they had the Court thing. Niall could be out of pocket for hours, and when he was done, that meant Savage would be, too, and on his way home. That could make things ugly. I needed to get my stuff out of here, and then meet with him on neutral ground, maybe in town somewhere. But how was I going to get into town?

I considered the Cadillac in the garage, but how shitty would that be? Leave him without a word *and* steal his car? Both would be temporary, but I didn't want to deal with that, either. I had two other people's numbers available to me on business cards. Melaina wasn't an option, though, not after her not-so-subtle threat about breaking her brother's heart. I didn't think Savage and I were close enough for it to be that bad, but any bit of hurt would have been enough for the female hellhound. The other card belonged to Addie. She was definitely my safest bet.

"Thanks for coming," I said as we loaded my suitcases into the back of her Jeep.

She shrugged. "No problem. And don't worry, I won't ask any questions."

My heart ached as we pulled away from Savage's cabin, but it was a pain I would have to endure. Before Addie had arrived, while I searched to make sure I had all of my belongings, nostalgia had already set in—and a longing for something I could never have. He and I could never have. It's strange how much we can grieve for something that never was more than a figment of our imagination—an unfulfilled wish, a dashed dream, a desire for what could have been but never was.

"Okay, I lied," Addie said as we came to the end of the road at the bottom of the mountain, about to turn onto a main street into town. "I have one question, but it's not about him. It's about you, and I'm dying to know—how was it to shift again?"

My head swiveled toward her in surprise. "How—?"

"Witchy senses." She laughed at my expression as she made the turn. "I felt it last night."

"You *felt* my shift? Wait. I thought you don't pay attention to anyone unless there's trouble." It was a good thing she'd brought this up, because if she—or anyone else—knew what happened last night, Savage, Niall, and whoever else were about to get into a lot of trouble if they lied to the Court.

She shrugged. "We don't. But I was kind of hoping you would shift while you were here. I could tell from your energy that it'd been a long time, and this is a safe place—as long as there are no humans around. So I guess subconsciously, I was feeling for it. And honestly, it was kind of a big fucking energy jolt and no doubt you."

I turned to look back out the window. Shit. "Did anyone else notice?"

"Not that I know of. Nobody's said anything. No alert went out or anything. I think your secret's still safe."

That was the second time I'd been told that today. But I had a lot of experience with secrets not being kept that way.

"So how was it?"

I couldn't help my smile, even with everything else that had happened. "It was kind of nice."

"Kind of nice?" she echoed. Stopped at a light, she peered over at me with a brow raised above her black-framed glasses.

"Okay, okay. It was unbelievable. She was happy to be free. Unfortunately, I was afraid of being seen, so she didn't get to be out for long."

The light changed, and we moved on, heading into the town square area.

"You could do it again. You could do it a lot here," she said as we passed by the coffee shop and bookstore.

I sighed. "I don't think so. I'm not like other shifters. Not even like other kelpie. I can't be seen by anyone—not humans or anyone else. In fact, the supes are more dangerous for me. Besides, I'm not staying long."

She turned and pulled into the parking lot for Whisper Falls Inn, a large and beautiful Victorian manor that sat catawampus on the corner, facing town square, a line of cottages behind it. She pushed the gear into park and turned in her seat to look at me.

"Like I said, I'm not going to pry. Any more than I already have. But don't leave because of him. I know he can be an asshole. Trust me. I fucking *know*. But you can still be here. I lived here my whole life and barely knew of him until recently. There's a lot this town has to offer, especially for someone like you. *Haven* is in the name for a reason."

I blew out another sigh. "My life is at home. I need to get back to it."

Needing to stop the conversation there, I opened the door and slid out.

Addie met me at the back of the Jeep. "Michaela's my BFF, and she owns the inn. I'll make sure she gives you a good deal."

Fifteen minutes later, Addie and her vampire best friend had me settled into a nice suite on the second floor. The inn was beautifully decorated, boasting a perfect combination of modern amenities while honoring its historical roots—the plaque by the front door said it was built in 1854, and that was a lot of history for this part of the country. My room contained a queen-sized sleigh bed, an armoire with a television inside, and a small writing desk in front of the window that looked out at the town square. It was feminine and beautiful, and more my style, but I already missed the masculinity of Savage's cabin.

Sighing and blinking back tears, I pulled out my sketch pad and sat on the bed. I'd intended to work on a new one-piece design, but without realizing it, I'd sketched an image of Savage. Damn it. Getting over him was going to be impossible. At least, until I left town and forgot him completely. That couldn't come soon enough.

Another vampire, a sassy redhead named Sindi, brought my dinner to my room, and I ate while writing a blog post, trying to keep my mind distracted. Later, my phone rang, showing Savage's number. I pressed the Ignore button. A couple of minutes later, it rang again: Niall.

"Where the fuck are you? Are you okay?" he demanded angrily as soon as I picked up. I could hear Savage yelling in the background.

"I'm fine. I'm at the inn."

Niall blew a harsh breath into the phone. "God damn it, Reyna. You had everyone in a fucking panic."

"Sorry. I thought you'd know."

He said something to Savage about calming down, then I heard footsteps followed by a door opening and closing and wind in the background. When he spoke to me again, he'd calmed down. "I came to get you, Rey. You couldn't wait a few hours?"

"For Savage to get there first?"

"You need to tell him. He was worried as fuck. Possibly more than I was. And now he's goin' to be fookin' mad."

"I will. Tell him that I'm okay. That I needed space, but I'll see him soon."

"Lie?" he asked.

"Unless you're ready to leave town right now, it's not a lie."

"Ach. We can't go, love. It's not safe for you out there."

"It's not safe here. You saw what happened last night."

He made a dismissive grunt. "That was a fluke."

"Yeah, well, I almost killed someone because of a fluke."

"You almost killed someone because he deserved it."

"I didn't know that, though!"

"Your kelpie did. I can see it clearly," he said. "As soon as you saw him, your kelpie knew something wasn't right about him, yeah? She knew he needed to die. Otherwise, she would have turned and run. She definitely wouldn't have let him get close enough to touch her, unless his arse deserved the outcome. *You* wouldn't have let him, Rey."

My mouth opened and closed, and I pressed my fingers to my forehead. "Our instinct is to kill."

"Our instinct is to draw out the evil and then kill, love. Only then. And I imagine yours is even more fine-tuned, considering what you are. The only other time the kelpie *has* to kill is in self-defense."

I rubbed my scar at the hairline in the center of my forehead. "Then why did Pops say I'd want to kill anyone I saw?"

"To scare you off from shifting. He knew you wouldn't want that guilt, so it was a way to force you to learn control."

The line fell silent for a moment as I let that sink in.

"Listen, love, I gotta talk to Savage before he destroys his own house. You're safe here. Relax. SIN-NO is dealing with some internal shit, and we're still tracking others who know about you. It's going to be a while before we can leave. Plus, I gotta do my part for the Havenwood Falls club. Getting them to protect you didn't come free, you know. At least, not at first." There was a loud crashing sound from his end of the line. "Gotta go!"

The call ended. I stared at the phone in my hand for a long while, still wrapping my mind around what he'd said about my kelpie's instincts and Pops lying about it. Guilt pricked my heart for being so mad at him when he died. He'd really done everything he could to keep me safe, even if his trust had been in the wrong place. Tears stung my eyes, and for the first time, I cried for him—ugly, loud sobs—missing him more than ever.

Then I cried for Savage.

My phone blew up with calls from him, but I ignored them. The next morning I awoke with puffy, swollen eyes to one message from him:

Just need to know you're ok. Tell me that and I'll leave you alone

I texted him back that I was and tossed my phone on the bed. Blowing out a heavy breath, I swung my legs out of bed to shower and dress. I had one night to feel sorry for myself, and it was over. Time to move on. He obviously was.

Knowing I had a lot to do for my business, I focused on work for the next two days, barely leaving my room except to grab something to eat in the inn's restaurant. My ears perked up every time I heard a motorcycle, and I found myself glancing out the window to see if it was him. His size alone would make him easy to pick out from most people, but I never saw him.

On the third day, there was a knock on my door.

"According to a little birdie, you've barely left your room. I thought you were on vacation," Addie said when I opened the door. "Instead, you're cooping yourself up in here and *working*."

I snorted. "I assume your birdie drinks blood."

"Among other things. Like coffee. But she's ditching our standing date today, so come join me for a cuppa joe. And a scone. Have you tried Coffee Haven's blueberry scones yet?" She licked her lips as though tasting them. "I won't take no for an answer."

I sighed. "Fine."

Grabbing my jacket and purse, I followed her downstairs, and we walked down the street to Coffee Haven.

"Oh, good. Willow's here. She has special blends for us special people, if you know what I mean."

A petite woman with silvery-blond hair turned from the espresso machine, her turquoise gaze falling on us. She smiled and came over to the long marble counter that looked like it belonged in an old-fashioned soda shop. "Hey, Addie. The usual?"

"Witch's Brew, yes, please."

"And for you?" The woman turned to me, her eyes narrowing. I sensed that she was fae—the light kind, possibly Seelie. Could she sense me, too? "I bet you'd like a Unicorn Fart."

I spluttered. "*Excuse me?*"

She and Addie both laughed.

"Their reactions get me every time," Willow guffawed, and Addie nodded, holding her belly from laughing so hard. The fae's expression eventually sobered. "Sorry. It's a special drink we recently started offering." She leaned in and whispered, "It's magical." She wiggled her fingers and winked before straightening up. "It's colorful, too. My 14-year-old cousin Dalton named it. It's really good, though, if you like vanilla and a bit of mocha." She leaned in again, once more whispering, "And a little extra energy boost."

"Oh, um, I think I'll just have a grande vanilla latte."

Willow laughed and pointed at the menu board. "Try again."

Her subtle reminder we weren't at Starbucks. Her drinks' names and flavors were much more interesting, and I took my time studying them.

"Oh, for fu—" Addie started before Willow cut her off.

"Language," Willow warned.

Addie sighed. "For *goddess's* sake, just get the Unicorn Fart. You know you want it. It's really good, especially with the scones."

I sighed. "Okay, fine." I smiled at Willow, but she stared at me expectantly. "You're going to make me say it, aren't you?"

"Where's the fun if you don't?"

I laughed, shaking my head. "I'll have the Unicorn Fart, please."

Willow gave a warm smile. "Now that wasn't so bad, was it? We women need to ask for what we want more often, no matter how ridiculous it sounds, you know?"

She winked again before turning away to make our drinks.

The next day, Addie stopped by to invite me to lunch at Napoli's. Afterward, she showed me the ice skating rink at the park and offered to teach me to ski or snowboard, my choice. The following day, she and Michaela asked me to join them for drinks.

"We usually go to the Dirty Knuckle," Michaela explained as Addie drove us. She was turned in her seat to look back at me, trying to keep my attention on her. That usually wasn't hard because she had the most amazing grayish-green eyes that pulled you in, but I had a hard time because we were headed in the direction of Savage's cabin. My heart had picked up speed. "But uh, SIN's usually at the Knuckle."

Now she had my attention. Biting my lip, I nodded in appreciation.

"I also wanted to show you something," Addie said as we made a turn that took us away from Savage's road. My relief was short-lived. As we ascended the side of the mountain, the road twisting and turning its way up, I felt the magical pull of the other night. We were near the falls.

"I'm not sure about this," I said, apprehensively. What if I lost control again?

Addie caught my gaze in the rear view mirror. "I am."

We turned into a parking lot of a large log cabin with a sign that said *Fallview Tavern & Grille*. The inside was cavernous, with an almost dungeon-like vibe, but in a comfortable and nice way. Not formal, but far above a hole-in-the-wall biker bar. There was a lot of wood and ironwork, which I found interesting, considering the fae population. Although I barely felt it, a benefit of the tattoo's magic, according to Addie. But that's not what had my attention. The view of the falls right beyond the outside patio had me mesmerized, my veins thrumming.

"Can you feel it?" Addie whispered from behind me, her head so close to mine, her mouth was nearly on my ear. I nodded. "I figured you could. There's aether in the water—an ancient kind of magic. It calls to you, doesn't it?"

"Like no other water does," I admitted. "Which is saying a lot."

"But you're stronger than it. You're stronger than anything that tries to control you." Her fingers twitched in front of us as her lips moved silently, and she must have done a muffling spell, because now she rocked back, her voice nearly normal. "When I was little, I was taught how magic can try to control us witches, if we let it, but that we have to be stronger and learn to control it instead. Because once we can, the power works *for* and *with* us—we use it, rather than the other way around. So I sat by the falls for hours every day until I learned how to control their effect on me. Until I learned how to absorb that power and make it mine." She leaned forward again, twisting her head to look at me intently. "That's how you gain your freedom and independence, Reyna. Empower yourself, and then use that power to make the choices *you* want. It doesn't matter where you are or who you're with. You're free as long as you have that power within."

I looked over my shoulder at her, dazed by her words of wisdom.

Her brows jumped, as a small smile curved her lips. She whispered again, "You didn't hear that from me. If you try to say otherwise, I will vehemently deny that there's any magic in those waters until my dying day. It's not meant for everyone to know. You won't find anything like these falls anywhere else, though. I *can* guarantee you that."

I was lost in thought the rest of the evening, barely paying attention as Addie and Michaela introduced me to some of the locals whose names I'd never remember, and checked out some of the tourists. When their conversation turned to weddings and fiancés, I completely tuned out, because my heart couldn't take it. I focused on what Addie had said instead, concentrating on the buzz of the magic in my veins and taking control.

The next day, I was happy to see her when she knocked on my door.

"I need a favor," I said, motioning her into my room.

"What's up?" She glanced around before settling her gaze on me.

"You gave me special protection in my tattoo, right?" I waited for her to nod. "Can you make it work outside the wards? So that I can leave and still be safe?"

She frowned. "I don't know . . ."

"Please, Addie. I know you've been trying to get me to stay, but I can't. I need to go home, and the sooner the better, but Niall won't let me. I can't be here any longer, though. It hurts too much. And you were right last night—about taking control. This is what I want. I want to go home."

She gnawed on her lip. "I'm really not supposed to, but there might be something I can do. But first, I need to show you something."

I groaned. "You've shown me so much, and I really appreciate it, but you're not going to convince me to stay. Why do you care so much?"

She shrugged. "I like you. I like your aura and your energy. And I want you to be safe. It's not perfect here. Trust me, I know. But this place is specially made for people like you." I began to shake my head, but she held up a hand. "Just let me take you one more place. It's a beautiful day for January, I have to go out there anyway, and I think you'll like it. And then, you do what you need to do. What you think is best for you, and I'll help however you need me to."

"One more place on the grand tour of Havenwood Falls?"

"Just one more. I promise. And you probably shouldn't wear those shoes."

I changed into my hiking boots, which Savage had rescued from the pond, grabbed what I needed, and headed out with her. I'd already learned that she preferred to walk everywhere around town, so when she led me to the Jeep, I knew we'd be going beyond the town proper. We drove for a while, turning off the main road and pulling up to what looked like commercial horse stables. A man stood by one of the fences, watching a teenager walk her horse around a large pen. He was tall, with midnight skin, short-cropped black hair, and muscles bigger than tree trunks. He might have possibly been bigger than Savage.

"Avalar," Addie called out as we walked toward him. She was right —it was a pretty nice day for January, causing the ground to squish in a muddy, slushy mess. The unseasonable temperatures wouldn't last long, though, according to the weather reports calling for plenty more snow.

The man she'd called Avalar turned. "Addie Beaumont. Thanks for coming."

"I hear you have someone in need of some ink."

His eyes cut over to me, black and cold. "And you are—" He paused, his nostrils flaring as he turned completely toward me. His head cocked to the side. "I know exactly who you are."

I glared at Addie. She threw her hands up, palms out. "Don't worry. It's okay. He's . . . like you."

I shook my head. "Can't be."

"Not quite," he said at the same time. "But she's right. I won't hurt you—unless you give me reason to." He looked back at Addie. "You said you were bringing someone I could trust."

She lifted her chin, not missing the accusation in his tone. "You can. I guarantee she'll bring neither you nor the others any harm. She's no threat. She only needs to see."

He considered me again, his gaze studying me from head to toe. His nostrils flared. Finally, he lifted his chin and bit out, "Fine. But don't make me regret this, Addie Beaumont."

He called out to someone to come keep an eye on the girl walking the horse, then he led us through the horse barn. When we came out on the other side, magic zapped through me—the zing felt like that of the town's protection wards when Savage and I had crossed over on the motorcycle.

My breath caught at the sight before us—on this side of the magic, unicorns galloped around the field.

CHAPTER 11

"*I* thought I was the only one," I said with wonder.

They were breathtaking—three horses colored periwinkle, magenta, and mint green with long horns and flowing manes and tails. They appeared to be racing each other around the field.

"You're the only one like you," Avalar said from my side. "Unless I'm completely wrong, you're a kelpie, too, aren't you?"

I peeked over at him. "Yeah. How did you know?"

"I sense my kind in you, but your kelpie side is stronger. Our kingdoms in Faerie neighbor each other. My great-grandmother told stories about one of our kind leaving the herd to go live with the kelpie and how ever since, there was a black unicorn that roamed the worlds —Faerie and now this one—every few hundred years. Black is the only color we don't see in our herd. Like ours, your kingdom was decimated by war, and those who were left came to this realm. Also like us, I believe your herd has scattered to all parts of this world?"

My hand pressing to my chest, I nodded. "Many of the stories had been lost among our kind. So that's how I have a horn? I'm a crossbreed?"

"There must have been a certain amount of magic involved, too.

Our kinds can't normally reproduce together. I'd heard tell of one like you long ago. I didn't realize there was another."

Staring at the unicorns in the field, I frowned. "We can't reproduce. That's why we never know who will be the next one, not even in which family."

"That must be part of the magic. I don't know much about it. Just the stories that were passed down."

"So these unicorns . . ." I gestured toward the field.

"I'm the leader of the herd. I'm trying to collect them in one place again. Here, by Havenwood Falls. It's the safest place I've found on this earth for us. You surely understand the dangers for our kind in this world. And if the Seelie-Unseelie War in Faerie spills over into our kingdom, or gods forbid, into this world, we should all be together. With some help from the Luna Coven, we have this cloaked field, private and secure, where we can shift and stretch our muscles, so to speak."

I watched them run, their heads thrown back as they whinnied— the sound of joy. Of security. Of freedom.

"That was a dirty trick," I grumbled to Addie on our way back to town, after she'd given Avalar's most recent arrival a registry tattoo.

She shrugged. "Well, you weren't getting it through your stubborn head that you belong here. I have no idea if you belong with Savage or not, Reyna, but I feel it in my gut that you do belong in this town. And you know what they say about a witch's instinct."

"What?"

She looked over at me, square in the eye. "Never question it."

As we closed in on Havenwood Falls, the rumble of motorcycles came from behind us.

"Maybe it's coincidence that they've been following us for several miles, or maybe you're being tailed," Addie said, after glancing up at the mirror.

I turned around to look out the back window. Two motorcycles followed us, the riders clad in black. I didn't recognize the front one, but the second guy was definitely Niall, his beard blowing in the wind.

"Yeah, probably being tailed." I turned back around, a lump in my throat.

"That looks like Liam out front."

Liam and Niall. Not Savage. Of course. I turned around to verify, and the man in front surely wasn't big enough to be Savage. The lump dissolved, but my heart hurt that he hadn't wanted to be part of my security detail. I had to admit, if only to myself, I missed his inherent need to protect me.

"Well, if you still want my help, you know how to reach me," Addie said as she pulled in front of the inn. "But you do what you know is right for you."

Climbing out of her Jeep, I nodded and gave her a wave just as the two bikes pulled up, rumbling loudly. Addie took off, and the engines cut, the sudden silence nearly deafening for a moment. Both guys swung off the bikes, Niall removing his helmet and sunglasses before opening his arms for me.

"You remember Pirate," he said as he hugged me.

I nodded, but said nothing. Liam stood there for a moment, his hands on his hips, his face downward, but his eyes still covered, so I wasn't sure where he looked. When he lifted his head, I assumed he was looking at me, but I couldn't feel his gaze—not like I could Savage's.

"Look," he started, his voice raspy. "You got our protection no matter what, and this normally isn't my thing, but I gotta say it. Savage is my brother, in all the ways. Maybe not blood, but we've spilled plenty of it together to count." He scratched his head as it turned away for a moment. "I've never seen him like he is now. Last week, he reminded me of a Tychon I knew long ago, but hadn't seen in centuries. Not since Anna. He changed after her—not for the better, mind you—then got worse after Lyra. But now . . ." He rubbed his head again, and then his neck, his mouth twisting. "Look, I need our guys ready to do what needs to be done, and Savage always has been. But I don't need any loose cannons. Especially not him. I don't like him like this, Reyna. Last week, he was my old friend. Now, he's fucking lethal. And I don't want to have to escort his ass back to Hell and have to leave him there, if you catch what I mean."

I crossed my arms, tilting my head. "It can't be about me, though. I don't think he cares. Not that much."

Liam peered at me through his glasses, focused enough that I could now feel it. "Trust me. He fucking cares. More than I've ever seen him care about anything or anyone in over three hundred years of knowing him."

With that, he swung his leg back over his bike and fired up the engine. Not knowing what to say, I just stood there and watched as he took off again.

"We need to talk," Niall said, his arm still over my shoulders as he steered me toward the inn's entrance.

"What is this? An intervention?" I muttered.

He didn't answer, didn't say anything at all until we were up in my room. Even then, he only looked around at first, picking things up to inspect, brushing his fingers over the décor. He finally turned around and nodded.

"This place suits you."

I shrugged. Savage's place, masculine yet warm and comforting, like him, had grown on me—like he had.

My throat felt thick at the thought, and I swallowed. "So what do we need to talk about? Are we able to finally leave?"

Leaning against the wall, he crossed his arms over his chest. He looked so out of place, all leather and chains and heavy boots in my lovely little room. Staring at me, he frowned.

"Is that what you really want?" he asked.

"I want to go home."

He sighed. "New Orleans isn't safe, love. SIN-NO is fucked up. One of the pledges gave you up, and they're findin' other arseholes who have snaked their way in. I really don't want to go back there, meself. And honestly, we don't think it'll ever be safe for you again."

I sucked my lips between my teeth to keep from scowling and lifted my chin. "It's my home, Niall. I hear what everyone's saying. And a part of me would love to stay. But I miss home. I miss my life."

One of his dark brows arched upward. "And what's there now to make it home, lass? What's left? *Who's* left?"

I sucked in a breath, clapping my hand over my heart. "Ouch!"

He stood up and strode over to me, picking up my hands. "I'm sorry, love, but it's the truth. Pops is gone. What else is there?"

I looked around the room, as though the walls here would give me answers. "I don't know. My apartment. My friends. Everything I know and love. You—right?"

He rolled his eyes. "Of course. I go where you go. But your apartment is gone. Went up in flames right after we left. You knew you couldn't go back there, anyway. Your friends? Axle's been watching your old account records. Nobody's called you, Rey. And are you sure *everything* you love is there?"

Pulling my hands from his grip, I turned my back to him.

"Reyna, it's not safe. If you really want to leave, we can go anywhere but there."

I spun back around. "I don't want to go anywhere else! Nowhere is going to be safe for long, Niall. I don't even know if this place will be. But I'm done living out of fear! They're not going to scare me away from my home, god damn it!"

"Well, good then, lass. Don't live in fear." Niall ducked his head to look me in the eyes with his piercing sapphire ones. "But you'd better think real hard about what truly scares you. Are you goin' home to face one fear—only 'cause you're runnin' from a bigger one?"

He left me gaping at him, but as soon as the door closed, I sank onto the bed and dropped my head into my hands. Then after a while, I lay back and stared at the ceiling. And then I decided to fuck my rule of one night to grieve and let myself cry again. But this time was all for Pops and the life he'd tried to give me. The life we could no longer have, ever again.

He was really gone. He wasn't going to show up in a bar in the Quarter or come knocking on my apartment door. But if he did, or if he showed up here right this very moment, I knew what he would tell me. What he would want me to do. Hell, he and Niall had already tried to get me to come out here once.

I didn't know what time it was or how long I'd been sobbing before my eyes dried and I blinked up at the ceiling. My room was dark, and so was the window. Night had fallen, but how long ago remained a mystery. I rolled over and searched blindly for my phone.

It was nearly midnight. I blew out a sigh and pulled up the text app. If I was going to stay here, make this town my home, I had to overcome my real fear. Damn Niall for being so astute.

Me: Are you busy?

It took a moment for his reply to come, long enough to have me panicking that he wouldn't talk to me anymore.

S: On a job

Me: Liam told me to call you

S: Liam needs to mind his fucking business

Me: Was he wrong then?

S: Probably

My heart sank.

S: What did he say?

I hesitated, then swallowed my fear, empowered myself, as Addie had said, and charged forward.

Me: That you care

Me: About me

S: . . .

S: . . .

Me: If he's right, why did you let me go so easily?

S: . . .

S: . . .

S: Are we really talking about this over text?

Me: Well, I was going to go to your place but I don't have a car

S: Be there in a minute

Me: What about your job?

S: She just said she wanted to go home

Exactly a minute later, there was banging on my door, making me jump. I opened it, and Savage advanced on me, driving me into my room. He shut the door, hard enough to make the pictures on the wall rattle, without stopping until he had me up against the wall.

"I'm your job?" I asked breathlessly.

"I already told you—you're more than a fucking job." He looked down at me, then yanked his sunglasses off and really scrutinized me, his gaze tangible as it roved over my face, the carnal look in his eyes sending a shiver down my spine. "You're my everything, Reyna."

My heart skipped, and I blinked up at him. "Then why did you let me go so easily?"

"Why did you?" he growled back.

I cringed, then looked over his shoulder, unable to look at him, knowing the question was completely fair. "I . . . I was confused and . . . scared."

He gave a sharp nod. "Exactly. And you want your freedom and independence, so I was giving you that. I will give you anything you fucking want, even if it's not me."

My gaze flew back to his face. "I can't be your old lady, Savage. I can't be a possession that you own. Does it have to be an all or nothing deal?"

He leaned in, pressing his thick forearms against the wall, caging me in as he lowered his forehead to mine. "I need to fucking own you, Reyna. I need you to be *mine*. But not how you're thinking. I need to fucking own you the way you already own me—mind, body, heart, and soul. *All* of me is already yours. So yeah, it's all or nothing."

My heart raced as I stared up at him. His breaths came quickly, warm on my face, that oaky, smoky scent of his flooding over me. I could barely breathe myself, my head spinning with dizziness. My hands shook at my sides, and I pressed them against my thighs.

He waited patiently, lifting his head only enough to watch me. Could he see all the emotions rushing through me? He could surely hear my pounding heart. The vampires downstairs probably could. Because the strongest emotion of all was fear—and not of some unknown hunters who might be out there searching for me, not for what they would do to me if they ever caught me.

No, my biggest fear was of this man in front of me, of what *he* would do to me . . . to my heart.

I will not live in fear. I will trust in me, in him, in us. This is what I want.

My trembling hand lifted slowly and cupped the side of his face. His eyes falling shut, he leaned into it.

"If you intend to say goodbye, don't," he said. "Just tell me to leave."

I watched him, noticing how his body stiffened, bracing for the blow. "Tychon."

He didn't open his eyes, but exhaled a long, slow breath.

"Don't leave me," I whispered.

His lids flew open, his eyes bright as he looked at me for assurance. I nodded.

"Never," he growled, turning his face in my hand to kiss my palm. "You are mine."

Swallowing, I nodded. "I am yours."

Leaning up and into him, I tilted my head back. His lips crashed onto mine, his hands gripping my hips and pulling me closer, his fingers digging into my flesh. The way he kissed me, the way he held me, I thought he may never let go. I wasn't sure I wanted him to. Ever.

But the kiss slowed, then he broke it, but without letting go of his hold on me.

"I can't give you kids," he said roughly. "I won't do that to you."

I shrugged. "I can't have kids. But there are other ways to have a family . . . if we want one. That's probably a conversation for later, though. Much later."

He shook his head and chuffed. "My fucking unicorn."

I frowned. "You can't be calling me that. But why do you?"

One side of his mouth curled up. "You wrote in one of your blog posts about your dream mentor. That designer who's too close to perfect and you admire so much and wish you could meet just once because you know it will change your life. I'm pretty sure those were your exact words. But you wrote that you probably never will because the opportunities are so rare. You called her your unicorn."

I nodded, remembering the piece. Niall and Pops had been pissed, afraid it would give me away. That was years ago, long before I ever was discovered.

"So . . . you like my designs?" I asked, confused.

He rolled his eyes, then leaned in closely. "No, sweetheart, you're *my* unicorn. The one woman who's perfect for me, a once-in-a-lifetime experience. And I knew the moment I saw you in that dark room back in NOLA that you would forever change my life."

Oh, gods. My knees went weak.

"Tychon Savage," I breathed, "I am most definitely your fucking unicorn."

He studied me for a moment, his nostrils flaring, probably scenting the dampness between my legs. Then, breaking our embrace, he turned and threw open the closet, tossing my suitcases on the bed. With both hands, he yanked all my clothes out of the closet and threw them in one of the bags. I was too bewildered to protest at the way he treated my precious clothes. He emptied my drawers next, stuffing everything into the rest of my bags. When he was done only a few minutes later, he sent a text, stacked up all the suitcases by the door, and finally looked at me.

"We're going home," he rumbled, grabbing my hand and pulling me out the door.

"But my stuff . . ." I looked over my shoulder at my suitcases, but he was already closing the door.

"A prospect will bring them out." He hurried down the stairs, so fast I could barely keep up with him.

He said nothing more as we climbed on the motorcycle and he turned the engine over. His body heated, keeping me warm for the ride. The unusually nice weather had already turned, and I could smell snow on the air. When we arrived at the cabin and climbed off the bike, he grabbed my hand and led me inside. Once the door was closed, his body visibly relaxed, and he turned around to face me. Still he seemed surprised to see me standing there, in his house again. I heard the lock click into place behind him, before he strode toward me.

"Am I your prisoner again?" I asked, my voice lilting in a tease.

"No, I am yours," he rumbled before curling his large arms around me and pulling me into him.

My hands pressed against his hard chest, feeling the planes.

"Is this mine?" I asked.

"Yours," he rumbled.

Sliding my arms around him to move closer, I dropped one hand down to his ass, hard as a rock as I tried to give it a squeeze.

"And this?" I asked, leaning back to look up at him with a small smile.

He smirked and nodded. Then he grabbed my other hand, pulling it in between us and pressing onto the bulge in his jeans, nearly as hard as his ass.

I stroked my hand up and down.

"Oh, this is definitely mine," I declared as I gave a gentle squeeze. "All. Mine."

He growled. "Fuck yeah, it is."

And the next thing I knew, I was in his arms, and he was striding for the bedroom. I was naked by the time he dropped me to the bed. I lay back on my elbows, lifting my breasts and spreading my legs wide.

Looking up at him through my lashes, I purred demurely, "Now take what's yours, my savage beast."

And he did. He took, but he also gave. And gave, and gave, and gave. Until neither of us could give any more.

As we lay in his bed, thick flakes of snow drifting down beyond the window, I settled into his big, strong, secure, and comfortable arms, resting my head next to his. And I finally admitted it—*this* was home.

EPILOGUE

*D*eath is a part of life, and so is saying goodbye. For nothing is permanent in this world, and the only guarantee in life is that someday death will come, and so will the goodbyes. But they're the two things that make you feel most alive because they make you *feel*.

Two months ago, we buried Pops. I hadn't allowed myself to feel right away, and I hadn't allowed myself to say goodbye.

Two months ago, I met Tychon Savage. And he made me feel again. Because of him, I was able to say goodbye to Pops. Because of him, I was able to learn to live.

I'd been living a life of fear since I was twelve years old, and that wasn't truly living. It'd been so long, though, I hadn't known better.

Until I met Savage.

And now, as I watched him and my brother come through the door, laughing and carrying two cases of beer and a bottle of whiskey, my heart filled to bursting. A life of love—I knew it now. I understood it. I lived it.

"So?" Melaina asked from her seat on the sofa next to me as she eyed the guys.

We'd just been going over plans for a lingerie fashion show at Silk, her nightclub. She'd introduced me to Izzie Itzae, who owned

Pleasurez, an adult toy store in town, which would be handling sales at the show. Izzie and I were already in talks about partnering together in an online retail store for my lingerie and other designs.

"It's done." Niall turned, showing us his new patch on the back of his cut. The bottom rocker that had said New Orleans was gone, replaced with a bright white one with *Colorado* on it. "My arse is officially in SIN-CO."

Melaina and I cheered half-heartedly while Savage poured him a drink. She didn't like the club much more than I did, but we'd both accepted it as a part of our lives. And we were both glad that the club had voted for Niall to patch into it.

"So, now that you know we're definitely staying, are you two . . . ?" I nudged my shoulder against hers as she eyed Niall like she wanted to devour him.

She stood up and smiled down at me. "I don't know if he can handle this."

We laughed as she walked away. Niall plopped down in her place.

"She might be right," he muttered. "That lass is fookin' somethin' else. Or I should say, *someones* else."

This surprised me. "Really? I honestly thought she wanted—"

"Oh, she wants me. How could she not want a fine Scotsman like me?" He winked, then slouched down closer to me and lowered his voice to a soft murmur, his beard tickling my ear. "She's not like any woman I've ever met, Rey. Bloody amazin', she is. But she has lovers. Plural. And she wants more."

"That's right," Melaina called from the kitchen. He should have known she'd hear. "I don't know that there's ever enough for me."

Niall lifted his chin and grabbed his crotch. "You just need a bit of this, sugartits, and that'll be more than plenty."

A pillow flew across the room and slammed into Niall's head.

"Can you fucking not?" Savage growled.

"Yeah, let's not," I quickly agreed, needing to know no more. I changed the subject, turning to Niall. "So . . . the kelpies?"

"You really want to do this?" he asked.

I nodded. "I've thought long and hard about it, especially about what that Avalar guy said. He's right—the war in Faerie could spill into our realm. And if that happens, all hell could break loose. I want as much of my herd together as we can get."

"They'll expect you to be their queen."

"I know." I looked at Savage, and he nodded in support. "I can do this. I want to do this. Even if there is no war, our people deserve what we have here—a life where we can be who and what we're meant to be. What we want to be."

"Get it approved by that damn Court first," Niall said, "then I'll start reachin' out."

We didn't know how many would come, and because of the Court and the rules, it might not even happen at all. But I had to at least try. I owed it to my people.

After Niall and Melaina left, Savage pulled me into his arms and nuzzled his face into the crook of my neck. "You're already my queen. And my goddess. And my . . ." He seemed to falter as he searched for another word.

"Your unicorn," I supplied.

He nodded against my skin. "My fucking unicorn."

Yes, this was living. And I knew Pops and my parents were smiling at me from another plane, happy I'd finally found home.

We hope you enjoyed this story in the Havenwood Falls world featuring a variety of supernatural creatures. If you want to read more about Addie, she's in *Forget You Not* and *Lose You Not*, and she stars in *Break Me Not* and *The Collector: Awakening*, all in the main Havenwood Falls series. Read Melaina and Niall's story coming to Havenwood Falls Sin & Silk in Fall 2019.

Havenwood Falls is a collaborative effort by multiple authors.

Books in the Havenwood Falls Sin & Silk series:

Taming the Beast by Nadirah Foxx
Plans Laid Bare by JD Nelson
Shift of Fate by Victoria Escobar
Stolen Wishes by Victoria Flynn
Damned Allure by Justine Winter
Savage Salvation by Kristie Cook
Dark Seduction by Michele G. Miller & R.K. Ryals
Soul Laid Bare by JD Nelson
Stray With Me by E.J. Fechenda
Chase the Flames by Desiree Lafawn
Flirting With Death by Nadirah Foxx

Also try the signature line, Havenwood Falls, the historical paranormal line, Legends of Havenwood Falls, and stories from the local supernatural college in Sun & Moon Academy.

Stay up to date at www.HavenwoodFalls.com

Subscribe to our reader group and receive free stories and more!

ABOUT THE AUTHOR

Kristie Cook is a lifelong, award-winning writer in various genres, primarily New Adult paranormal romance and contemporary fantasy. Her internationally bestselling, award-winning Soul Savers Series includes seven books, as well as several companion novellas and short stories. Over 1.2 million Soul Savers books have been downloaded. She has also written The Book of Phoenix trilogy, a New Adult paranormal romance series. Her books have been featured in *USA Today's* HEA section, on Good Morning America, and in the Emmy's Gifting Suite.

Kristie also created, writes in, and publishes the award-winning Havenwood Falls shared world, a collaborative project with multiple series, dozens of authors, and countless stories.

Besides writing, Kristie enjoys reading, cooking, traveling, getting her hippie on, and feeding her addictions to coffee, chocolate, cheese, The Walking Dead, Game of Thrones, and Supernatural. She has lived in eleven states, but currently calls Florida home.

Email: kristie@kristiecook.com
Author's Website & Blog: http://www.KristieCook.com
Amazon: https://www.amazon.com/Kristie-Cook/e/B0046KG8R4?
tag=kriscook-20
BookBub: https://www.bookbub.com/authors/kristie-cook
Facebook: http://www.facebook.com/AuthorKristieCook

ACKNOWLEDGMENTS

Much appreciation goes to my parents, for supporting this crazy dream of mine and really being there when things get so hard, it seems impossible to go on. Thank you, thank you, thank you. But I really hope you never read this one.

So much gratitude to the Havenwood Falls Collective—our little family of authors, editors, and designers. I'm so glad you've joined me on this adventure and grateful for all you've done in growing, shaping, and molding this world. Sometimes I'm just overwhelmed and completely humbled that you've put your trust, time, and energy into me and this project. It's been so much work and so much fun so far. I hope you'll stick around!

Special thanks to R.K. Ryals, who helped create the hellhound lore and the SIN MC, and for allowing me to use Liam "Pirate" Peters. To Kallie Ross for the use of Willa, to Randi Cooley Wilson for Callie, to E.J. Fechenda for Willow, and to Megan Linski for Avalar. I know I dropped some other names and places that our authors created, so thank you all. Oh, and to Melissa Wright, for creating the SIN logo.

And last but far from least, thank you, dear reader, for giving me a few hours of your time for this book. I hope it was worth it. I'm always stunned that you love Havenwood Falls and the characters as much as we do. There's still much more to come so don't be a stranger. In fact, Addie's waiting for you to give you your tattoo.

AN EXCERPT

Dark Seduction (A Havenwood Falls Sin & Silk Novella) by Michele G. Miller & R.K. Ryals

He is tormented by the past. She is traumatized by her present.

Tied since birth to a darkness that longs to break free, spiritual psychic Harper Sinclair fights a never-ending battle with demonic spirits. Her only relief comes from the fallen angel whom she's long ignored deeper feelings for. Physically scarred and emotionally wounded from a year of fights and revelations, Harper is losing herself to the one thing she's always been afraid of: herself. And in the process, she's changing her relationship with the one friend she trusts the most.

Elias Jamison is a fallen angel. He lost his place in Heaven when he chose his friends over his creator. He fell, but he is not lost. For centuries, Elias maintained his innate goodness, fought against evil, and protected those in need—except for one. Grief-stricken, Elias pushed his loss aside for over one hundred years as he watched over the Freeman bloodline from afar, but the deeper his feelings grow for Harper Sinclair, the deeper old guilt digs in. Regret is a powerful tool when wielded against us, and vanquishing Harper's demons means confronting his own.

There's a little darkness in all of us. Are you ready to embrace it?

DARK SEDUCTION

BY MICHELE G. MILLER & R.K. RYALS

"Oscar Wilde," I whispered, the author's name rolling off my tongue, merely a breath in the middle of the night. The name was an odd thing to think aloud, but I'd been listening to an audiobook recently and, after the dream I'd just had, it was a Wilde quote I thought of as I locked gazes with myself in the mirror.

A dreamer is one who can only find his way by moonlight, and his punishment is that he sees the dawn before the rest of the world, I mouthed.

I thrived during the night, but I felt lost after the dawn. The darkness was my friend, the day my punishment for paying too much attention to the night. Hell, the darkness was my family, in the form of shadow demons and spirits. My constant companions.

My face was pale, my long brown hair a chaotic nest around my head, my eyes home to dark circles put there by too little sleep.

The bathroom mirror was too honest, telling me things I didn't want to know about myself.

As a spiritual writer who'd been brought into this world after my pregnant mother was stabbed by a necromancer's athame, I'd always been tied to darkness in one form or another. It was this gift that introduced me to the fallen angel who helped me understand myself and subsequently, the other fallen angel who became my closest friend.

It was Elias Jamison—my best friend—I thought of now, my gaze on my reflection. My breathing was too rapid, my heart pounding, beads of sweat clinging to my brow. All because I'd had a scorching hot, completely inappropriate dream about the man who'd slowly worked his way past my wall of defenses over the last year. I trusted him more than I did anyone else.

He'd helped save my life twice.

I wasn't an easy person to befriend. I was reclusive, but Elias didn't seem to mind. The way he checked in with me—the texts he often sent—was important to me. Which was why when he left recently, his absence affected me more than I thought it would.

Because you're angry, the spirits around me said bluntly.

"No," I argued. "It was good he left."

When Elias had disappeared on angel business, I honestly thought the distance would be good. I'd become too dependent on having him near. I needed to be more open with the friends I'd made recently, but while I'd become closer to the others in town the last year, especially after our recent alliance to battle against the one known as the Collector, it was still Elias I felt most comfortable with.

Until now. Until this dream. This was why I shouldn't sleep.

"Is this going to become a habit?" a snide voice asked. The bronze-barbed mace—he was basically a baseball bat on steroids—who lived with me bounced near the doorway, impatient and agitated. Desi—short for Destroyer—was a sentient weapon that shape-shifted into a huge lion with wings. He'd been a gift from the first and only lover I'd ever had. I didn't quite know what finally losing my virginity to a high-ranking fallen angel at twenty-three and being rewarded with a weapon said about me, but I was all about collecting odd experiences and memories.

Desi was annoying as hell, but I couldn't live without him. Some people spoiled their cats and dogs. I spoiled my ancient shape-shifting pet weapon. Go figure. He needed lots of love, attention, and validation.

"What woke you up this time?" Desi asked.

It wasn't a nightmare that had me this restless.

126

A red blush bloomed across my skin, and I turned on the sink to splash cold water on my face. Images of flesh on flesh, Elias's hands and lips in places I'd never imagined his hands and lips being before, burned into my subconscious. Elias was a big man, brawny and broad, a beard covering a handsomely rugged face. His voice was raspy, deep, and sexy in a rock star kind of way.

He'd called my name in the dream. Over and over again.

I stared at the running water, watching as it circled the drain and disappeared, the dream replaying in my head.

"Harper."

Elias breathed my name into my ear, surprising me, because I'd been asleep when he slid into bed behind me. His voice and the warm feel of his body woke me. I should have pushed him away, the shock of him being there bringing me to my senses, but all I felt was excitement and contentment.

"Finally," I whispered, because I wanted this. Really *wanted this.*

"Harper," he repeated, his arms pulling me into his embrace.

He was naked and hard. As was I—the naked part anyway—which was strange, because I didn't sleep naked. Tonight, however, there was only desire and need between us, his hand sweeping over the smooth contours of my stomach before slipping between my legs to caress me.

"You're wet," Elias said, satisfied.

His fingers slid through the moist heat to my clit, the sensation he caused with his touch so painfully pleasant that I almost lost it. My whimpers filled the room.

What was I doing? What were we doing?

"Elias—"

He stopped me with a kiss, rolling me over so quickly, I had no time to think before his lips crashed down onto mine, his tongue invading my mouth. His hand gripped my ass, our bodies pressed so closely together there was no space between us, the hard length of him hot against my belly.

"Tell me you're ready for me," he told me, pulling back to rest his forehead against mine, his breath fanning my lips.

"I'm ready."

He had me on my back in seconds, entering me quickly, as if he were afraid I'd change my mind. He filled me up completely.

"So tight," he growled.

His hips moved, and I lost the ability to think.

"Eli—"

I had woken on the verge of saying his name. My hand drifted to my stomach, the sudden tickle in my gut new and fresh and different.

"I want Elias," I heard myself say, my voice huskier and sexier than usual.

My eyes shot to the mirror, to the gaze staring back at me.

"What'd you say?" I asked myself. My free hand found my lips, my fingers tracing my mouth.

Desi snorted from his spot by the door. "Look what you've done to her. She's finally gone crazy," he said, his words directed at the dark spirits.

Shadow figures ducked in and out of the bathroom, ghostly images that played with my shower curtains and hissed at Desi.

Despite the chaos and their presence, the hand I had on my stomach drifted lower, and I jerked, forcing it up and away from my body.

"Out!" I yelled suddenly, my voice too rough. "All of you!" Embarrassment turned my skin hot, and I shooed the mace and ghostly shadows out the door before slamming it shut and turning to slide down to the floor. "Holy shit!"

I wasn't sure what bothered me more. The fact that I had been about to pleasure myself in front of a group of demonic spirits and a sentient weapon or the fact that I was about to masturbate while thinking about my best friend.

"What's going on with you, Harper?" I asked aloud.

The freaky thing wasn't me talking to myself or having sexy dreams about Elias. It's not like dreams could be controlled, and I talked to myself all the time.

It was the fact that I *answered* myself, my voice seductive when I said, "Being horny isn't bad. Not doing something about it is completely terrible for a person's health."

I knew what this was. This was me fighting with myself because part of me wanted what another part of me wasn't sure of, but fear and confusion shot down my spine nonetheless, immobilizing me. The last time I'd fought with myself like this, the last time I'd been this conflicted, was when I was taken captive by an evil doll—long story—and held in a creepy dollhouse for weeks in a nightmare that had ended with me physically wounded and emotionally bruised.

"No one understands you, Harper." The shadows returned, thick, dark, and seductive, their voices strong and powerful in my head. Their voices didn't sound like mine. I was used to their voices.

"But we understand you. We understand you like no one else ever will. We understand your desire and your needs."

Trembling, I slid back up the door and turned cautiously toward my mirror.

It was just me. The same plain Jane I'd always been—messy brown hair, scared green eyes, and a plaid pajama set that was two sizes too big.

This was the Harper I knew. Only there were dark forms crowded behind me, shadow people, their wispy, sinister arms outstretched as if to hug me.

"We are everything you will ever need and more."

Desi pounded on the bathroom door. "At least use the air freshener when you're done."

His light joke broke the tension, and the shadows scattered. A small, nervous laugh escaped me, my wide eyes dropping to my hands where they gripped the bathroom sink so tightly, the knuckles were white.

I felt like I was torn in two, completely divided between who I used to be and who I was tempted to be. I'd even started talking to myself in my sleep, getting up at night to leave written messages I found later. I'd once written a message in red lipstick on my mirror. It was hell to clean off.

Releasing the sink, I walked on unsteady, light feet from the bathroom, into the bedroom, and out into the kitchen. My hands were swifter than my brain, quick to make a cup of hot cocoa that I cradled in my palms, the warmth comforting.

Desi followed, quieter than he'd been before. It was hard reading him in weapon form. He didn't have eyes or lips. When he communicated, words were just *heard*. I didn't question how it worked. I was just glad he could speak, sarcasm and all, because he kept me from feeling lonely.

My mouth was full of hot chocolate when Desi murmured, "You feel different, and I don't think it's because you had a sex dream."

Holy hell!

Cocoa spewed everywhere. "You didn't just say that!"

"What did I say then?" he asked sweetly. "It's—"

"There are certain pet privileges you don't have."

"I'm not a pet," he spat.

Arguing was normal for Desi and me, but tonight it cloaked an entirely different problem. And it had nothing to do with dreams. I felt different. Antsy and impatient. As if my body was telling me I needed to *do* something.

My phone, which I rarely used because the signal tended to be bad in Havenwood Falls, lay on the kitchen counter, and I touched it lightly.

The urge to text Elias was strong, but I'd promised myself I wouldn't reach out to him until he returned. Elias had an entire life and problems of his own outside of me. Besides, it would be a little weird to text him after having an erotic dream about him, right? More so since it was the middle of the night.

I tapped the phone's screen and touched the messenger icon to scroll through our old texts. I was one of those people who never deleted anything.

Sweet memories surfaced, the messages a reminder of the first time I'd met Elias outside Coffee Haven. The day I realized he was open to befriending a naïve, shy girl who'd just experienced her first heartbreak and learned exactly how deep her ties to Hell and the spirit world went. Christmas in Havenwood Falls a year ago. Back when all I'd cared about was tackling a list of firsts.

A lot had happened in a year.

"You've got too much drama for being a loner. You need a fuck buddy." The moment the words left my mouth, my hands flew to my lips, my eyes widening.

Desi bounced up onto the counter, leaving scratches on the surface. He was going to ruin my house.

"Was that you?" he asked, incredulous.

It *was* me, but I was behaving differently than usual.

Me and *not* me.

"Because you have different needs now," the shadows revealed. *"Let go, Harper. Let go and be everything you were born to be. Listen to yourself."*

"Your eyes," Desi breathed.

Grabbing my phone, I clicked the camera icon and put it on selfie mode. My eyes were dilated, the black pupils completely overtaking the green.

"I'm pretty, aren't I?" I asked myself, a small smile lifting the corner of my lips.

Me and *not* me.

This me liked the way she looked in oversized plaid pajamas. She oozed a confidence about her messy hair and startled eyes that I lacked.

This me had a thing for fallen angel Elias Jamison, and she wasn't the kind to sit back and let him slide through her fingers.

"We know each other so well," I said aloud, my gaze on the camera. My finger pressed the picture key, my brows arched as it captured my image. "I should send this to him. I look good."

Was I possessed? All because of a sex dream? Did demons possess you if you had dreams about sex? Because if they did, the entire population was a walking exorcism project.

"Wow." Desi whistled. "You've officially lost your mind."

I didn't answer him because I was sending a picture text I wasn't sure I wanted to send.

Purchase **Dark Seduction** where books are sold.

www.ingramcontent.com/pod-product-compliance
Lightning Source LLC
Chambersburg PA
CBHW051956170626
46808CB00007B/2652